TOLD
UNDER THE
BLUE UMBRELLA

New Stories for New Children

Selected by the

LITERATURE COMMITTEE OF THE
ASSOCIATION FOR CHILDHOOD EDUCATION

Illustrated by
MARGUERITE DAVIS

NEW YORK
THE MACMILLAN COMPANY
1939

TO

THE CHILDREN OF TODAY

for

Their Enjoyment

CONTENTS

TOLD UNDER THE BLUE UMBRELLA

A companion volume to
Told Under the Green Umbrella

THE BLUE UMBRELLA

MARY JANE and her mother were at work. They had cleaned the bottom shelf of the closet. And they had cleaned the next to the bottom shelf.

> "Everything out,
> Wipe and clean,
> Clean and wipe,
> And everything in."

That is what they said as they worked.

But when they came to the third shelf of the closet Mary Jane couldn't help any more. She wasn't tall enough. She stretched her arms. She wasn't tall enough. She stretched her legs. Tiptoe, tiptoe, she stood as tall as she could. Still she wasn't tall enough. So her mother had to work alone to clean the third shelf.

"Everything out!" she said as she began. And out came the old blue umbrella. It was faded. Part of the handle had fallen off. One of its ribs was loose.

"We must have this old umbrella mended and a new cover put on it," said Mary Jane's mother. "It is too old and broken to be kept in our clean closet."

Mary Jane looked at the blue umbrella. She thought of something she would like to do with it. "Please,

Mother," she asked, "may I take it outside? I will call
Charles Edward. We can play with it." And her
mother said Yes.

Away went Mary Jane. Away went the blue umbrella with her. As she reached the sidewalk in front of
the house she called,

> "Charles Edward,
> Charles Edward,
> Come and play,
> See the umbrella
> We found today."

Charles Edward came running. His express wagon
came rolling along behind him. It rattled on the sidewalk as he pulled it along.

Mary Jane raised the blue umbrella to show it. A
shower of fine dust fell from its faded folds. But Mary

— 2 —

Jane was as proud as she could be. She marched up and down the sidewalk. She held the umbrella proudly over her head.

"My umbrella is blue," she said. "It is like the sky."

"Look out! Look out!" shouted Charles Edward. "Look out for my express wagon. It will run over you and your blue umbrella."

Mary Jane wasn't afraid of that. She held her blue umbrella too high. Up the sidewalk she went. Up the sidewalk went Charles Edward. Up the sidewalk his express wagon followed him. Then they all turned around. Mary Jane and her blue umbrella! Charles Edward and his express wagon! Down the sidewalk they all came. Up and down, up and down, they went like marching men.

"I will give you a ride in my express wagon," said Charles Edward. Mary Jane climbed in. She didn't leave the blue umbrella behind. Not at all. She held it over her head as she sat in the wagon.

— 3 —

Away went the express wagon. Away went Mary Jane and the blue umbrella.

"I am riding in a taxicab," said Mary Jane. "My blue umbrella is its top."

"Oo-oo-ga! Oo-oo-ga!" shouted Charles Edward. "Look out! Look out for the taxicab." He went so fast that the express-wagon taxicab almost tipped over when he turned it at the corner.

Then Charles Edward climbed into the wagon to have his turn at riding. He held the blue umbrella. Away went Mary Jane. She went so fast that the express wagon did tip over. Over and over Charles Edward rolled. Over and over rolled the blue umbrella. But Charles Edward wasn't hurt and the blue umbrella wasn't hurt, so they went on with their play.

They played and played until they were tired. Then they both sat in the express wagon and held the blue umbrella over their heads. Mary Jane told about cleaning the closet shelves. She told about how they found the blue umbrella.

"I wish Mother would let me keep this umbrella," she said. "I think it is too old for her to use. I wish I had it for my own. I like to play with it."

"So do I," said Charles Edward. "Ask your mother if she will let you have it to keep."

"Come on," said Mary Jane. "We will go and ask her now." They climbed out of the express wagon and started for the door.

Just then they heard the tinkling of a little bell. They stopped to listen.

"Tinkle, tinkle," said the little bell from around the corner. Mary Jane and Charles Edward ran to see what it was doing there. The blue umbrella went along. Mary Jane held it over her head. The express wagon went too. Charles Edward pulled it close behind him.

"Tinkle, tinkle, tinkle," said the little bell, as it came around the corner. A little old man was swinging it to make it tinkle. He had a pack of old umbrellas on his back.

"Tinkle, tinkle, tinkle," the bell kept on saying.

"Umbrellas! Umbrellas! I mend old umbrellas," said the little old man. Then he saw Mary Jane and the blue umbrella. He stopped short; he looked straight at the blue umbrella over Mary Jane's head. "I can make that old umbrella look like new," he said as he looked at it.

Mary Jane didn't want her old blue umbrella to look like new. She liked its faded blue cover. She liked its broken handle. She liked its loose rib. She wanted the umbrella mender to go away quickly, but her mother had heard the little tinkling bell. She had heard the little old man. As the little old man stood looking at the blue umbrella she came to the door.

—5—

"Let me mend the old umbrella, lady," said the umbrella mender to Mary Jane's mother.

"Oh, Mother," said Mary Jane running to her, "please don't have it mended. I like it. Charles Edward likes it, too. Please give it to us. We want to play with it."

Mary Jane's mother looked at her. She looked at the faded blue umbrella. Then she looked at the little old umbrella mender and she said to him, "No, thank you. We don't want the old umbrella mended."

"Tinkle, tinkle," said the little bell, as the umbrella mender went on up the street to try to find someone who did want an umbrella made to look like new.

Mary Jane and Charles Edward jumped up and down. They knew that they could keep the blue umbrella for their play. The express wagon rattled its wheels. The blue umbrella bobbed up and down with Mary Jane.

"Good-by, umbrella mender, good-by," they all seemed to say. "You need not come back."

Mary Jane said to Charles Edward as they began to play again:

> "The umbrella is ours.
> The blue umbrella is ours.
> We can walk under it,
> We can talk under it."

And so they did.

By James Tippett

BUILDING

BOBBY JOE had a little teddy bear. Teddy bear could say Oooh.

Bobby Joe took out his blocks. He put a block here and here and here and here. He put a block here and here, until he had made a . . . house.

"A house for my . . . teddy bear," said Bobby Joe.

Bobby Joe had a little brown cow. Little cow could say Moo, mooo.

Bobby Joe took out his blocks. He put a block here and here and here and here. He put a block here and here, until he had made a . . . house.

"A house for my . . . cow," said Bobby Joe.

Bobby Joe had a little pink pig. Little pig could say Eek, eeek.

Bobby Joe took out some more blocks. He put a block here and here and here and here. He put a block here and here, until he had made still another house.

"A house for my . . . pig," said Bobby Joe.

Teddy bear lived in *this* house. Little cow lived in *this* house. And little pig lived in the next.

"I have . . . one, two, three houses," counted Bobby Joe. And he had. One, two, three houses! One for the teddy bear that went Oooh, and one for the cow that went Mooo, and one for the pig that went Eek, eeek. A house for each had Bobby Joe!

By Dorothy Baruch

THE EXPRESS WAGON *

BOBBY JOE took out his express wagon and started to go for a walk.

He walked and he walked and he walked. He passed the kitchen steps and the laundry yard, and the telegraph pole.

He walked down a hill and over a bridge and up a hill. He walked and walked and walked. And then he came to the . . . park.

There he saw a little gray kitty.

"Miaow, miaow," went the kitty.

Bobby Joe thought she was trying to say, "Please give me a ride!" So he lifted her up onto his express wagon.

Off he started again with kitty sitting in the express wagon. He walked and walked. He walked back down the hill and over the bridge and up the hill on the other side. He walked back past the . . . telegraph pole, and the . . . laundry yard, and the . . . kitchen steps.

He walked and he walked all around the house to the front and away to the . . . corner. And there he saw a little brown dog. "Bow-wow," said the dog.

---

* The dots in the Bobby Joe stories suggest a pause to give listeners a chance to supply next word.

Bobby Joe thought he was trying to say, "Please give me a ride!" So he lifted him up onto his express wagon.

But no sooner was the doggie there than the kitty began to make a terrible fuss. She arched her back. She stuck out her claws. She went Sss-fwt, sss-fwt! and hit at the dog with her sharp, sharp claws, this way, this way, scratch, scratch, scratch.

"Bow-wow-wow-wow," went the doggie.

"Grrrrr," he went too.

"Sss-fwt," went the kitty, and "Miiii-aoow, miiii-aoow."

And before Bobby Joe could do anything at all, the kitty and the doggie jumped out and ran away.

And Bobby Joe went home alone.

By Dorothy Baruch

— 9 —

IN THE GRASS

BOBBY JOE looked down. He looked down into the green, green grass.

He looked. And he looked. He saw something, he did.

There was a spider in the green, green grass—a spider with oh, so many creepy, crawly legs! The spider was going through the grass—scitter scatter, scitter scatter. Oh, so fast through the grass! Until it was gone, all gone.

Bobby Joe looked. And he looked.

He saw something else.

There was a grasshopper in the green, green grass. The grasshopper was going through the grass—hop, hop, hop; hop, hop, hop. Oh, so fast through the grass! Until it was gone, all gone.

Bobby Joe looked. And he looked.

He saw something else.

There was a caterpillar in the green, green grass. It was fuzzy—very fuzzy! The caterpillar was going through the grass—hump, hump, hump. It moved so slowly, so very slowly! Hump, hump, hump, through the grass. Until it, too, was gone, all gone.

And still Bobby Joe looked and looked, down into the green, green grass.

At last he saw something else.

There was a ladybug—a bright red ladybug. But— the ladybug wasn't going through the green, green grass. It was standing still, quite still. And then, all of a sudden, *it flew away!*

By Dorothy Baruch

CINDER WAGON

(THE following experience, which the children identify as "Cinder Wagon" was written down practically as it occurred, in terms of the children's conversation. It is a "story" of recurrent interest to them, because it occurs repeatedly during the winter.)

Men came with horses and a wagon
And the wagon was full of cinders.
Why? Because snow came in the night.
Snow made the roads and paths so slippery
That people could not walk on them; so slippery
That cars could not go safely on them.
So men came with a wagon full of cinders.
They had shovels and buckets.
Men filled their shovels full of cinders.
They poured cinders into their buckets,
Shoosh-shoosh-shoosh—the cinders went into the
    buckets.
Men walked in the road, throwing cinders on the snow.
Black cinders they threw on the snowy roads and paths,
So that cars might run without skidding.

We watched the horses walking in the snow
Pulling the wagon load of cinders.
     "Look at us, horse,
       Stick out your pink tongue,
       Lift up your hoof, horse,
       So we can see your shoes.
       You have funny shoes—horseshoes
       Made of iron.
       We cannot see any toes on your feet.
       Your harness buckles jingle.
       Your harness is hooked to the cinder wagon
       So you can pull it through the snow."

We watched men throwing cinders on the snow.
With scoops they lifted cinders from their full buckets,
And scattered them on the snow.
Chu-chu-chu-chu—he walks through the snow
Throwing cinders on the path:

Chu-chu-chu-chu—until his bucket is empty.
Bang! He bumps his bucket with his scoop.

One man stays in the wagon to drive,
He sits on the edge of the seat to rest.
    "Good-by, horses!
      Come again on a snowy day.
      Good-by, men with wagon load of cinders!
      Come when it snows.
      Put cinders on the paths,
      Put cinders on the roads.
      It helps people."
By Katherine Reeves

LITTLE SHEEP ONE, TWO, THREE

ONCE upon a time there were Little Sheep One, Two,
Three. They were hungry little sheep.
  So they walked
        walked
           walked along
  and they walked
        walked
           walked along
  and they walked
        walked
           walked along
until they came to a meadow where the grass grew
green.

  All day long they nibbled
        nibbled
          nibbled the grass

and they nibbled
        nibbled
            nibbled the grass
     and they nibbled
        nibbled
            nibbled the grass
until they had eaten so much grass that they couldn't
nibble another bite.

Then Little Sheep One, Two, Three were thirsty.
  So they walked
      walked
      walked along

— 14 —

and they walked
    walked
       walked along
  and they walked
    walked
       walked along
until they came to a cool stream that flowed through the
meadow where the grass grew green.

The Little Sheep drank
      drank
        drank of the water
  and they drank
      drank
        drank of the water
  and they drank
      drank
        drank of the water
until they had drunk so much water they couldn't drink
another drop.

Then Little Sheep One, Two, Three were sleepy.
  So they walked
    walked
      walked along
  and they walked
    walked
      walked along
  and they walked
    walked
      walked along
until they came to a large tree that grew in the meadow
where the grass grew green.

They lay down and they slept
                        slept
                            slept all night
                and they slept
                        slept
                            slept all night
                and they slept
                        slept
                            slept all night
until it was morning and they were so rested that they
couldn't sleep another wink.

Then Little Sheep One, Two, Three woke up and spent
another day
            walking along
                    nibbling the grass
                            and drinking the water
in the meadow where the grass grew green.

By Marjorie Allen Anderson

WALKING IN THE WOODS

We went walking in the woods together:
Leaves were scarlet, leaves were brown;
It was fun, in the sunny weather—
Squirrels darting,
Woodchucks scampering,
Acorns dropping,
Brown birds chattering.
Earth was frosty to our feet,
Smell of pine was sharp and sweet;
We held pine cones in our hands,

We touched snow berries on a stem,
But we did not gather them.
We brought home some silver moss,
We brought home a creamy fungus,
We brought home some colored leaves.

It was fun when we walked together,
Walked in the woods in autumn weather—
Walked in the woods in sunny weather:
All of us liked it,
All of us thought it was fun.

By Katherine Reeves

LOST IN THE LEAVES

PATSY lived with her mother and her daddy and her little dog Bing.

One morning when Patsy looked out of the window she saw the red and gold and brown leaves falling from the trees. "Oh, Mother," she called, "may I play in the leaves?"

"Yes, Patsy, you may play in the leaves," said Mother.

"Bow-wow-wow," barked Bing, as if to say, "I want to play too."

Patsy put on her little green cap, and she put on her little green sweater. Then she and Bing started out to play.

As they left, Mother gave Patsy a rake and said, "Patsy, would you like to rake all the leaves into one big pile for me?"

"Yes," Patsy answered, "I would like to rake the leaves."

"Bow-wow-wow," barked Bing, as if to say, "I'll help you rake the leaves."

Patsy and Bing had a happy time playing in the leaves. Patsy raked up a pile of golden leaves; she raked up a pile of brown leaves; she raked up a pile of red leaves. Then she raked them all together into one big pile. Just as she had finished, Bing scampered up and jumped into the center of the pile, and the leaves covered him over. Then Patsy jumped into the pile beside Bing, and the leaves covered her too.

Soon Mother came out to help Patsy. She saw the pile of red and gold and brown leaves, but she could not see Patsy or Bing anywhere. She looked behind the rosebush; she looked up and down the street; she even looked in the garden, but no one was there.

"Yoo-hoo! Yoo-hoo! Patsy, where are you?" she called.

Patsy kept very still under the pile of leaves.

Mother called again "Yoo-hoo! Yoo-hoo! Patsy, where are you?"

But Patsy kept very still and did not make a single sound.

"Yoo-hoo! Patsy, Bing, where are you?"

"Bow-wow-wow," barked Bing from under the pile of leaves. Then out he jumped, wagging his stubby tail as if to say "Here I am."

"And here I am too," cried Patsy, laughing as she jumped out from the leaves.

Then Mother knew that Patsy and Bing had not been lost at all, but had only been hiding just for fun.

"Thank you, Patsy," she said, "for raking the leaves. Thank you, Bing, for helping Patsy."

Bing wagged his stubby tail, as if to say, "I like to help Patsy rake the leaves."

By Frances Rowley

THE BLOCK TOWER

(THE building blocks were bought of a little old lady with twinkling eyes. She had to sell, besides the building blocks, pony reins, dolls, velocipedes, balls, a blue and gold tea set, a gay tin horn, and a green wagon with red wheels. The children called her the Toy Lady.)

Some of the building blocks were bought for a child who knew how to make all sorts of things with them: barns and bridges and palaces and churches.

He was always thinking of something new to build. Once it was a tunnel for a train to go through, and another time it was a steamboat; and one day he said he would build a tower as tall as he was.

"Don't you think that will be splendid?" he asked his mother.

"Yes indeed," said she, "and hard too."

So the little boy set to work piling the blocks one on top of another. Soon the tower was knee high, waist high, chest high; that was just the way the little boy and his mother measured it.

"It will soon be as tall as I am," said the little boy, but he had hardly spoken when down the blocks fell!

The little boy thought that the wind which was coming through the nursery window had blown the tower

down, and his mother thought it might have fallen because he had been in such a hurry; but, anyway, the little boy said he would build it up again, and make it stand too.

Up, up, up the tower climbed.

"It's chin high now. Look! Look, Mother!" he called, but before Mother could turn her head, down came the blocks!

The little boy began to think that he could not build such a high tower after all, but his mother still thought he could. Even though the blocks had fallen twice, she believed he could do it.

"As tall as I am?" asked the little boy.

"As tall as you are," said his mother.

So the little boy set to work once more piling the blocks one on top of another and taking pains with every one. Soon the tower was knee high, waist high, chest high, chin high, as high as the little boy's nose! But it didn't fall, not even when he put one more block on it and another one still. And then——

"It's taller than I am," called the little boy. "Hurrah!"

He thought the tower was the very finest thing he had ever built. So did his mother.

By Maud Lindsay

PELLE'S NEW SUIT

THERE was once a little Swedish boy whose name was Pelle. Now, Pelle had a lamb which was all his own and which he took care of all himself.

The lamb grew and Pelle grew. And the lamb's wool grew longer and longer, but Pelle's coat only grew shorter!

One day Pelle took a pair of shears and cut off all the lamb's wool. Then he took the wool to his grandmother and said: "Granny dear, please card this wool for me!"

"That I will, my dear," said his grandmother, "if you will pull the weeds in my carrot patch for me."

So Pelle pulled the weeds in Granny's carrot patch and Granny carded Pelle's wool.

Then Pelle went to his other grandmother and said:

"Grandmother dear, please spin this wool into yarn for me!"

"That will I gladly do, my dear," said his grandmother, "if while I am spinning it you will tend my cows for me."

And so Pelle tended Grandmother's cows and Grandmother spun Pelle's yarn.

Then Pelle went to a neighbor who was a painter and asked him for some paint with which to color his yarn.

"What a silly little boy you are!" laughed the painter. "My paint is not what you want to color your wool. But if you will row over to the store to get a bottle of turpentine for me you may buy yourself some dye out of the change from the shilling."

So Pelle rowed over to the store and bought a bottle of turpentine for the painter, and bought for himself a large sack of blue dye out of the change from the shilling.

Then he dyed his wool himself until it was all, all blue.

And then Pelle went to his mother and said: "Mother dear, please weave this yarn into cloth for me."

"That will I gladly do," said his mother, "if you will take care of your little sister for me."

So Pelle took good care of his little sister, and Mother wove the wool into cloth.

Then Pelle went to the tailor: "Dear Mr. Tailor, please make a suit for me out of this cloth."

"Is that what you want, you little rascal?" said the tailor. "Indeed I will, if you will rake my hay and bring in my wood and feed my pigs for me."

So Pelle raked the tailor's hay and fed his pigs.

And then he carried in all the wood. And the tailor had Pelle's suit ready that very Saturday evening.

And on Sunday morning Pelle put on his new suit and went to his lamb and said: "Thank you very much for my new suit, little lamb."

"Ba-a-ah," said the lamb, and it sounded almost as if the lamb were laughing.

By Elsa Beskow

THE FEEL OF THINGS

ONE sunshiny day in summer Frank was ready to play out-of-doors. "Mother," he said, "it is so hot. I should like to take off my shoes and socks."

"Very well," Mother replied, "you may take them off."

Quickly Frank sat on the floor and untied the lace of one shoe. He loosened it—there, and there, and there. Then he took hold of the heel of the shoe and pulled and pulled. Off came one shoe! Then Frank untied the lace of the other shoe. He loosened the lace carefully— there, and there, and there. Then he took hold of the heel and pulled and pulled. Off came that shoe!

>Off came one shoe,
>Off came two!
>Frank loosened it,
>Frank pulled it,
>He knew what to do.

Next Frank took hold of the top of one sock. He pushed it down over the heel and over the toe and one sock was off. He wiggled his toes and stretched them. Then Frank took hold of the top of the other sock. He pushed it down over the heel and over the toe and another sock was off. He wiggled those toes and stretched them. How comfortable it was to have shoes off and socks off this warm, moist day. Frank stood up.

Sock off the heel,
Sock off the toe,
Frank is ready,
Off he'll go.

First Frank stepped on the mat before the door. The mat was rough. It scratched his toes. It pricked his feet. So Frank sang,

"Rough mat,
Prickly mat,
Scratchy mat there;
I feel you, mat,
I like you, mat,
Because my feet are bare."

Next Frank stepped on the porch and down the steps. The wooden steps were warm, for the sun had been shining on them all the long morning. So Frank sang,

"Wooden steps,
Warm steps,
Sunny steps there;
I feel you, steps,
I like you, steps,
Because my feet are bare."

"And now I'll go a little farther," said Frank. Then he walked on the gray stone path. The path was shady. It felt cool. His feet made a little sound "pat, pat, pat. pat" as he walked. So Frank sang,

"Pat, pat,
Cool path,

Smooth path there;
I feel you, path,
I like you, path,
Because my feet are bare."

"And now I'll go a little farther," said Frank. Then
he walked on the soft, green grass. The grass was cool.
It tickled his toes. His feet made no sound. Then Frank
sang,

"Cool grass,
Soft grass,
Tickly grass there;
I feel you, grass,
I like you, grass,
Because my feet are bare."

"What fun it is to be barefoot," said Frank, as he
walked back over the cool, shady path and up the
warm, sunny steps and on the rough mat into the house.
There stood his shoes. They could not take a walk without Frank's feet in them. There lay Frank's socks. They
could not take a walk without Frank's feet in them. So
Frank sang them a little song and here it is:

"I like to feel the mat,
Rough mat,
Scratchy mat,
With my feet,
My bare feet,
My bare, bare, bare feet.

"I like to feel the steps,
Warm steps,
Sunny steps,
With my feet,

My bare feet,
My bare, bare, bare feet.

"I like to feel the path,
Smooth path,
Cool path,
With my feet,

My bare feet,
My bare, bare, bare feet.

"I like to feel the grass,
Soft grass,
Tickly grass,
With my feet,
My bare feet,
My bare, bare, bare feet.

"Bare feet, bare feet,
Bare, bare, bare feet;
I stretch my toes,
I wiggle my toes,
I feel with the toes
Of my bare, bare feet."
                          By Mary G. Phillips

ROXY AND THE ROBIN

THERE was once a duck who lived in a pen. He had smooth white feathers and orange feet, and his name was Roxy.

Roxy had a tub of water in his pen, and he swam in his tub every day. When the children filled his tub with cool, clean water in the morning he could hardly wait

for his swim. Into the tub he hopped; round and round he swam, paddling with his orange feet, dipping his orange bill, ducking his smooth white head under the water, and washing his smooth white feathers.

How he liked his swim. The water made his feathers shine until he was as white as milk. When he finished his swim he preened his feathers, and flapped his wings, and walked about in the sunshine on his orange feet.

In the elm tree beside his pen some robins had made

a nest. When the baby robins were big enough to leave their nest they flew down beside Roxy's pen. Sometimes they pecked at his food through the wire netting of his pen. Roxy did not like the robins very well. They made too much noise. When they flew near his pen he went behind a box and stayed there until they went back to their nest.

One day a strange thing happened. The door to Roxy's pen was left open. Roxy was walking around in the sunshine when he heard a noise behind him. What do you think it was? One of the baby robins had hopped right into his pen. Just then the wind blew the door shut, and the baby robin was caught in Roxy's pen. Roxy made a funny quacking sound. Then he waddled to the corner behind his box and looked over the top at the baby robin.

The baby robin did not know what to do. He tried to fly up to the nest in the elm tree, but the wire netting of the pen stopped him. He hopped on the ground, from one end of the pen to the other. He made the chirping sound that made his mother fly down from the tree and try to help him. But she could not help him. The mother robin was on the outside of the pen, and the baby robin was on the inside of the pen, and there was no one to open the door. Roxy quacked, the baby robin chirped, the mother robin made her calling sound, but the baby robin could not get out. He flew against the wire netting and bumped his head. He flew against the wire netting and bumped his wings. He hopped on the ground and tried to get out, but he could not.

Jane was just waking from her nap. From her window she saw the baby robin struggling and fluttering and beating his wings against the pen. He was trying so hard to get out. Jane saw Roxy behind his box. She saw the mother bird flying outside trying to help her baby.

The duck did not know what to do. The mother robin did not know what to do. The baby robin did not know what to do.

But Jane knew what to do. She put her shoes on quickly and ran outdoors to Roxy's pen. She opened the door wide. Then what do you think happened? The baby robin flew right out of the pen. He was so glad to be free. He flew straight up to his nest. The mother robin stopped making her calling sound, and flew up to the nest. Roxy came out from behind his box, and walked in the sunshine on his orange feet.

Jane shut the door very carefully, and went to tell her mother all about it.

By Katherine Reeves

JIM AND SCOTCH AND THE LITTLE RED WAGON

ONCE upon a time it was Jim's birthday. He was four years old. (Just as old as you, and you; and older than you, and you, and you; but not so old as you, and you.)

Jim got up early because it was his birthday. When he had eaten his breakfast his father said, "Jim, there's something in the back yard for you in a basket."

Jim hurried out the back door. There on the grass in the back yard was a big basket. Over the top of the basket Jim could see two little pointed ears and the tip of a furry tail. It was a puppy! A real, live, collie puppy!

Jim lifted him out of the basket. The little dog sat on

Jim's lap and licked Jim's hands with his soft little pink tongue.

"He's a Scotch collie," said Jim's father.

"Then I'll name him Scotch," said Jim.

"I think Scotch is hungry," said Jim's mother. "We'll give him some milk in a saucer."

"Will that be enough for him?" asked Jim.

"Yes," said his mother. "He isn't big enough to have meat and vegetables yet, but if we give him milk every day he will grow to be big."

So Jim gave Scotch milk in a saucer every day. Scotch lapped up the milk with his little pink tongue and grew and grew. He grew so much that one day Jim's mother said, "I think Scotch is big enough to have some vegetables and just a small piece of meat."

After that every day Jim put some vegetables and a little meat in Scotch's saucer and he scooped it up with his little pink tongue. Scotch kept on growing. His legs grew long, his tail grew long, and he was covered with long hair that was light brown, except around his neck, where it was pure white. His nose grew long and pointed. His tongue grew long, but it was still soft and pink.

The days went by, and the days went by, until it was Jim's birthday again. This time he was—how old? He was five years old.

Jim got up early because it was his birthday. While he was eating breakfast he said, "I think this ought to be Scotch's birthday too."

"All right," said Father, "after breakfast you will find something in the back yard for you and for Scotch."

As soon as he was through eating, Jim called Scotch and hurried out the back door. There on the grass in the back yard was a shiny little red wagon!

"It's a very nice wagon," said Jim, "but how is it for Scotch too?"

"Look at it very carefully, Jim," said his father. "Is it just like your old yellow wagon?"

Jim looked very carefully. The little red wagon seemed to look just like the old yellow one (except that the color was different). It had four wheels—two on each side.

"But," said Jim, "look here—why does it have two handles?"

Sure enough, fastened on the front of the wagon there were two long straight pieces of wood—one at either side.

"These are not really handles like the one on your old yellow wagon," said Father. "You see, this wagon is made like the big ones that horses pull, and those pieces of wood are called 'shafts.'"

"Oh, Father, do you suppose Scotch could pull this little red wagon?" asked Jim.

"Yes, I believe he could," said Jim's father.

"Then that was why you said the wagon was for him too!" said Jim. "But can we make him pull it? He doesn't know how."

"We'll have to teach him," said Jim's father, "and I'll tell you how."

He had Jim get some heavy string and then he said, "Now, call Scotch, and get him to stand in front of the wagon between the shafts."

When he was there, Jim patted him and kept him

still while his father put the string around him just a certain way and tied it to the shafts.

But after Scotch was all harnessed to the little red wagon, he just stood there and licked Jim's hand with his long pink tongue. When Jim walked away and called Scotch to follow him, Scotch started to run as he always did. But the little red wagon was fastened to him and it felt heavy, so he stopped and stood looking at Jim.

"How will we ever make him pull the wagon?" Jim asked his father.

"I think I know a way," said Jim's father. "What does Scotch like especially to eat?"

"Well," said Jim, "he likes cookies."

"Go ask Mother for a cookie, then," said Father.

When Jim came out with the cookie in his hand his father said, "Break off a piece of cookie, then stand a little way in front of Scotch and call him. When he comes to you, give him the piece of cookie."

So Jim broke off a little piece of cookie and held it out and said, "Here, Scotch! Here, Scotch!"

Scotch started to come and the little red wagon that was fastened to him felt heavy, but he smelled the cookie and he wanted it. So he tried very hard and he pulled the wagon just a little way. Then Jim gave him the piece of cookie and it was very good.

"Now, walk along a little farther and call him again," said Jim's father.

So Jim walked along. Then he broke off another piece of cookie. He held it out and called, "Here, Scotch! Here, Scotch!" This time Scotch knew he could make the little red wagon come along with him if he tried hard enough, and he did. Jim gave him another piece of cookie.

Then Jim walked along some more. He held out another piece of cookie and called Scotch. He kept walking along breaking off pieces of cookie and calling Scotch until pretty soon Scotch had pulled the little red wagon all the way across the back yard.

"Now I think he has learned to pull the wagon," said Jim's father. "You won't have to give him pieces of cookie every little way."

And sure enough, after that when Scotch was harnessed to the little red wagon he would follow Jim all around the yard. Jim and Scotch and the little red wagon played together all summer.

By Marie Louise Allen

THE STORY OF DOBBIN

DOBBIN was a wooden horse. He belonged to Jane and Jerry who were twins four years old. He had belonged to them ever since they were tiny babies and they had played with him so much that now he was almost worn out. Poor Dobbin! One leg was broken, one eye was gone, and so were his mane and tail. The wheels had come off his little red wooden stand. Most of all Dobbin needed a coat of paint.

One evening Father brought home a new wooden horse. It was larger than Dobbin. It was all shiny with paint and had a fine black mane and tail. The twins were so pleased that they danced about and clapped their hands.

"What shall we do with Dobbin?" asked Jerry.

"I think we might send him to a little boy who has no toys to play with," said Mother. "But, of course, we can't send him just the way he is. We must paint and mend him."

So the twins helped Mother mend Dobbin. First

they mended the broken leg and put four new wheels on his stand.

Then Mother let them take turns painting Dobbin a beautiful gray, and the stand bright red. Last of all Mother took the paintbrush and gave Dobbin two black eyes, a bridle, a black mane, and some black spots. With the red paint she gave him a red saddle.

"Now he is all ready," said Mother.
"But he has no tail!" said Jane.
Mother took some hairs from an old broom and glued them in the place where Dobbin's tail had been.

The hairs were quite short and Dobbin's new tail was so straight and stiff that it made the twins laugh to look at it.

When all the paint was dry, Mother said, "Now we can wrap Dobbin up and send him to his new home." She found a large sheet of paper, stood Dobbin on it, and began to tie up the package. Jane and Jerry watched. Soon there wasn't any Dobbin to be seen— not even the straight, stiff, little tail.

"Oh, Mother," cried Jane, "we can't send Dobbin away. He's been with us such a long time."

"Send the new horse instead," said Jerry.

Mother looked surprised, but she opened the package and put the new horse in Dobbin's place.

Jane and Jerry hugged Dobbin. "We like you ever so much better than the new horse," they told him. Then they took turns riding on his back as they had always done.

"Gee up, Dobbin! Whoa, Dobbin!" they shouted.

Dobbin ran so fast on his little red wheels that it seemed as if he knew he was to stay and play with the twins for a great many more years.

By Alice Dalgliesh

NOTE: The four first pictures of Dobbin can be drawn easily by the teacher as she tells the story.

ANGUS AND THE DUCKS

ONCE there was a very young little dog whose name was Angus, because his mother and his father came from Scotland.

Although the rest of Angus was quite small, his head was very large and so were his feet.

Angus was curious about many places and many things:

He was curious about what lived under the sofa and in dark corners and who was the little dog in the mirror.

He was curious about things-which-came-apart and those things-which-don't-come-apart, such as slippers and gentlemen's suspenders and things like that.

Angus was also curious about things-outdoors but he could not find out much about them because of a leash.

The leash was fastened at one end to the collar around his neck and at the other end to somebody else.

But Angus was most curious of all about a noise which came from the other side of the large green hedge at the end of the garden. The noise usually sounded like this: Quack! Quack! Quackety! Quack!! But sometimes it sounded like this: Quackety! Quackety! Quackety! Quack!!

One day the door between outdoors and indoors was left open by mistake; and out went Angus without the leash or somebody else.

Down the little path he ran until he came to the large green hedge at the end of the garden.

He tried to go around it but it was much too long. He tried to go over it but it was much too high. So Angus

went under the large green hedge and came out on the
other side. There, directly in front of him were two
white ducks. They were marching forward, one-foot-
up and one-foot-down.

Quack! Quack! Quackety! Quack!!

Angus said:

Woo-oo-oof!!!

Away went the ducks all of a flutter.

Quackety! Quackety!

Quackety! Quackety! Quackety!!!

Angus followed after.

Soon the ducks stopped by a stone watering trough
under a mulberry tree.

Angus stopped, too. Each duck dipped a yellow bill
in the clear cool water. Angus watched. Each duck
took a long drink of the cool clear water. Still Angus
watched. Each duck took another long drink of cool
clear water.

Then Angus said:

Woo-oo-oof!!!

Away the ducks scuttled and Angus lapped the cool
clear water.

Birds sang in the mulberry tree.

The sun made patterns through the leaves over the
grass.

The ducks talked together:

Quack! Quack! Quack!

Then:

Hiss-s-s-s-s-s!!! Hiss-s-s-s-s-s!!!

The first duck nipped Angus' tail!

Hiss-s-s-s-s-s!!! Hiss-s-s-s-s-s!!!

The second duck flapped his wings!

Angus scrambled under the large green hedge, scurried up the little path, scampered into the house and crawled under the sofa.

For exactly *three* minutes by the clock, Angus was *not* curious about anything at all.

By Marjorie Flack

PADDY'S THREE PETS

ONCE upon a time there was a big fat father who had a fat little boy named Paddy. One evening, when fat Father came home from the office, he wiped his feet on the mat, opened the door with his jingly key, and whistled. Down the stairs ran fat Paddy as fast as his short legs would carry him—paddity-pat, paddity-pat, paddity-pat. First he hugged Father then he put his hand into one of the big overcoat pockets. And what do you think he pulled out? A white guinea pig with pink eyes.

"Squeak! Squeak! Squeak!" cried the guinea pig.

"What will you do with him?" asked fat Father.

Fat Paddy stroked the soft fur of the little guinea pig. "I'll give him some lettuce and play with him," he replied. And so he did, until the guinea pig grew fat and fatter.

— 43 —

One evening, when fat Father came home from the office again, he wiped his feet on the mat, opened the door with his jingly key, and whistled. Down the stairs came fat Paddy as fast as his short legs would carry

him—paddity-pat, paddity-pat, paddity-pat! First he hugged Father then he put his hand into one of the big overcoat pockets. And what do you think he pulled out? A little gray kitten with white paws.

"Miaow! Miaow! Miaow!" cried the kitten.

"What will you do with him?" asked fat Father.

Fat Paddy stroked the soft fur of the little gray kitten. "I'll give him some milk and play with him," he replied. And so he did, until the kitten grew fat and fatter. Paddy and the guinea pig and the kitten all played together.

One more evening, when fat Father came home from the office, he wiped his feet on the mat, opened the door with his jingly key, and whistled. Down the stairs came fat Paddy as fast as his short legs would carry him— paddity-pat, paddity-pat, paddity-pat. First he hugged Father then he put his hand into one of the big overcoat pockets. And what do you think he pulled out? A little brown puppy with one black ear.

"Bow-wow! Bow-wow! Bow-wow!" cried the puppy.

"What will you do with him?" asked fat Father.

Fat Paddy stroked the soft brown puppy. "I'll give him some milk and play with him," he replied. And so he did, until the brown puppy with one black ear grew fat and fatter.

One Sunday morning fat Paddy, the fat guinea pig, the fat kitten, and the fat puppy were all playing together on the sunny porch. It was a quiet day. No grocer's wagon rumbled over the street. No children's feet skipped and scuffled on the way to school. Far away fat Paddy heard the church bell.

"Ding-dong! Ding-dong! Ding-dong!" it called and

that meant "Come to church! Come to church! Come to church!"

Fat Paddy scrambled to his feet and gathered his pets gently in his arms. He said to them, "It is time for me to wash my face and hands and put on my best suit and new shoes, for I am going to church with Father. I will put you, fat guinea pig, and you, fat kitty, and you, fat puppy, in a warm, cozy place for a nap."

Hanging in the hall was fat Father's overcoat. Into one deep, warm pocket he put the kitten; into another the guinea pig; and into the inside pocket, dark, deep,

and warm, he squeezed the puppy. Then fat Paddy went upstairs—up one step, up two steps, up three steps, up, up, up, up went his feet to the very top.

When he was quite ready for church he came down the stairs—paddity-pat, paddity-pat, paddity-pat—and there was fat Father waiting for him in the hall. Fat Father had on his overcoat. The pockets bulged and were quite heavy, but then Father's pockets always did bulge, and they always were heavy, for he kept lots of nice things in those pockets. Fat Paddy was thinking of his own best suit and his own new shoes. He did not remember what was in those deep, warm pockets.

Around the corner fat Father and little fat Paddy walked together and their feet kept time with the bell, which was calling again: "Ding-dong! Ding-dong! Ding-dong! Come to church! Come to church! Come to church!"

Fat Father and little fat Paddy walked together into the church and up the wide aisle. They walked very quietly with hushed feet, for the church was still. At one pew they stopped and fat Paddy sat down. Fat Father took off his coat and put it over the back of the seat. Bump! went the fat guinea pig's sides against the pew.

"Squeak! Squeak!" cried the guinea pig, waking from his nap.

Quickly fat Father picked up his coat, but he did not see the guinea pig. The people sitting near by smiled. Fat Father turned the coat around and again put it over the back of the seat. This time the kitten's fat sides went Bump! against the pew. The gray kitten woke up.

"Miaow! Miaow!" cried the kitten.

People near by smiled again and so did Paddy. Father did not smile. He was puzzled. Where did the sound come from? Once more he picked up his coat. This time he squeezed the fat sides of the brown puppy. The puppy awoke from his nap.

"Bow-wow! Bow-wow!" cried the puppy.

More people smiled and Paddy leaned over to Father and whispered, "They are taking their naps in your pockets."

Fat Father smiled at Paddy and whispered back, "Home is the place for naps. I'll take them home and come back." Then fat Father picked up his coat very carefully and walked softly down the aisle.

And after that the guinea pig with pink eyes, the gray kitten with white paws, and the brown puppy with one black ear each had a little box in the garage for naps.

By Mary G. Phillips

SNOW WHITE

(SNOW WHITE was a baby chicken. She was hatched into a flock of white leghorn hens on Broadview Ranch in Oregon. Peggy owned the ranch.)

The first thing that little Snow White knew was waking up in a tight, dark little room and wishing to get out. Tap, tap, went little Snow White's bill against the wall. Tap, tap, tap, tap! It was hard work, so she went to sleep and had a long nap. But the hard wall had cracked just a little.

When Snow White woke up, a little breath of air was coming through the crack she had made. She felt very big and strong. Tap, tap, tap, tap, went her little bill, and she turned quite around in the narrow room, tapping all the time. Tired out, she went to sleep again, but she had made a crack quite around the room.

When she woke up again, *stretch* went her two little feet! *Snap* went the wall of the little room, and out rolled little Snow White. Right out into a crowd of a hundred little brothers and sisters she rolled. Like herself, they were dressed in the silkiest yellow down. And all of them were saying "Peep-peep," very softly; for they were warm and sleepy.

"Peep-peep," said Snow White—then she had another long nap. When she woke up, sunlight was streaming through a little round window into the tiny house in which she found herself. The tiny house was an incubator. Snow White got up on her little feet, which were not quite strong and fit, and ran about with her hundred little brothers and sisters.

Then Peggy came and opened the door. She took them all out in a big basket, and they saw the blue sky and the juniper trees and the sagebrush bushes of Broadview.

By Alice Day Pratt

(PEGGY built a box nest for Snow White. Snow White laid the first of her many eggs to help Peggy run Broadview Ranch. Pax was a collie dog.)

"Ca-a-a-a-a—caw-caw-caw-caw—ca-aaa!" sang Snow White.

Long, long ago she had lost all of her yellow down and had become dressed in beautiful, smooth, snow-white feathers. Just lately her little comb had been growing wonderfully and was bright, coral red.

"Ca-ca-ca-ca-ca-ca-caw!" she sang over and over.

Peggy looked at her. By and by, when the work in the cabin was done, Peggy came out to the chicken house with some boards, a saw and hammer, and some nails. She worked for several hours.

When she had finished, there was a row of little boxes up against the wall. Then Peggy brought out a long piece of canvas and hung a curtain over the boxes, so that it was all dim twilight inside of them. Then she went to the load of straw, which she had hauled the day before, and took enough to make a soft, deep nest in each box.

"Ca-a-w, ca-ca-ca-ca-ca-caw!" sang Snow White and her sisters, walking in and out of the new boxes. "Ca-aw, ca-ca-ca-ca-ca-caw!"

One morning early, Snow White went into the box that she had chosen for herself, settled down on the soft nest, and stayed for a long time. When at last she came off, she came with a great uproar. "Cut-cut-cut-ca-da-cut!" she shouted. "Cut-cut-cut-ca-da-cut!"

Peggy came out. "What is it, Snow White?" she asked.

"Cut-cut-cut-cut-ca-da-a-cut!" answered Snow White.

Peggy looked behind the curtain. There, in Snow White's nest, was a beautiful snow-white egg.

"Snow White has laid the first egg," said Peggy to Pax.

"Cut-cut-cut-cut-ca-da-a-cut!" shouted Snow White.

By Alice Day Pratt

SAGEBRUSH BABIES

(BROADVIEW was a brand-new homestead ranch in the sagebrush country of central Oregon. Peggy was its owner. Rab was her dear and faithful saddle pony. Pax was her collie dog who took charge of everything and everybody night and day.)

Mother Sage Rabbit was a long way from home. For weeks past she had hardly moved out of sight of a certain little bower of wild shrubs on a steep ridge of the Broadview pasture. Feed was not very good on that ridge, and she had been getting thin and hungry. Today she had decided that it was time for her to go out into the world again to hunt for better living. Back to the old wheat field she had come. It was spring, and all over the field volunteer wheat was pushing up, green and tender. Mother Rabbit was having a rare time. She hopped about daintily, cropping only the richest and juiciest spears. Now and then she took a bite of tender Jim Hill mustard and now and then a little flower. There had been plenty of rain lately, and everything was tender and delicious.

By and by, feeling quite satisfied, she sat straight up and looked for a long minute over the landscape. Nothing was moving anywhere. Mother Rabbit laid her ears close back against her neck and shot off across the pasture like a streak of light. When she reached the rocky ridge, she sat up behind a bunch of sage and looked out in every direction for another long minute. Then, with her ears laid back, she raced up the ridge and disappeared under a cascade of lovely pink and white shrubs.

Away back about the base of these shrubs there was plenty of room. Mother Rabbit had set up a home there some weeks ago. She had scooped out a little basin and lined it with grass and fur. Cuddled close together,

with their ears laid back and their bright eyes wide open, were six baby sage rabbits. They were beautiful little things. Mother Sage Rabbit was crazy about them. Now she made as much fuss about them as if she had been gone for a week. She bathed them all around, cuddled them close, and gave them a good dinner of rabbit milk.

When the babies were all asleep, Mother Rabbit crept out to the edge of her bower, intending to dress her own coat from nose to tail. As it turned out, she didn't dress a hair. She saw something that brought her little heart up into her very mouth. Racing up the ridge, head on for the flowery bower, came Pax with his nose to the ground. He was right on her trail—the trail that she had made only fifteen minutes ago.

Anyone seeing Mother Rabbit might have thought her paralyzed with fright, she sat so still. But Mother Rabbit was doing her best thinking. When Pax's hot breath was almost upon her, out she darted, right under his nose, and made off up the ridge. It looked to Pax like the best chance he had ever had yet. Here was a rabbit with no start at all and seemingly not able to run very fast. She kept just a few feet ahead of him. The warm smell of her made him crazy. For when Pax was hunting, he was not a gentle ranch doggie, he was a wolf.

Pax and Mother Rabbit were far out of sight when Peggy came up to the beautiful flowering shrub. She and Pax had started out to find Rab. She stopped to enjoy the lovely pink and white sprays and to put her nose down to them. It was while her face was down among the branches that she caught sight of the least little movement underneath. She bent lower. There were the six little rabbits with their twelve big bright eyes fixed upon her face and their little noses noise-lessly wiggling to take in a scent that was quite new.

It was very funny. Peggy would have loved to pick up one or two of them, but she was afraid of frightening them out of their shelter, and she thought of Pax. She went on quietly, looking for Rab. Half a mile farther on Pax joined her, panting terribly and almost worn out. At the same time Mother Rabbit was already at home again, sniffing the scent of a human who had been within a foot of her babies and, as she thought, failed to see them. She was very much amused. But Peggy had the laugh on Mother Sage Rabbit.

By Alice Day Pratt

THE LITTLE BLUE DISHES

ONCE upon a time there was a poor woodcutter who lived with his wife and three children in a forest in Germany. There was a big boy called Hans and a little boy named Peterkin and a dear little sister named Gretchen, just five years old. Christmas came and the children went to the toy shop to look at all of the toys. [Enumerate toys.]

"Gretchen," said Peterkin, "what do you like best?"

"Oh! that little box of blue dishes," said Gretchen. "That is the very best of all."

On Christmas Eve the children hung up their stockings, although their mother had said that they were so poor they could not have much this Christmas. Hans ran out after supper to play with the big boys. Gretchen and Peterkin sat talking before the fire about the Christmas toys and especially about the box of blue dishes. By and by Gretchen ran off to bed and was soon asleep. Peterkin ran to look in his bank. Only one penny, but he took it and ran quickly to the toy shop.

"What have you for a penny?" said he to the toy man.

"Only a small heart with a picture on it," said the man.

"But I want that set of blue dishes," said Peterkin.

"Oh, they cost ten cents," said the man.

So Peterkin bought the candy heart and put it in Gretchen's stocking and then Peterkin ran off to bed.

Pretty soon Hans came home. He was cold and hungry. When he saw Gretchen's stocking he peeked in, then put his hand in and drew out the candy heart. "Oh," said Hans, "how good this smells," and before you could say a word he had eaten the candy heart. "Oh dear," he said, "that was for Gretchen for Christmas. I'll run and buy something else for her," so he ran to his bank and he had ten pennies. [Count pennies.] Quickly he ran to the toy store.

"What have you for ten pennies?" he asked the store-keeper.

"Well, I'm almost sold out," said the toyman, "but here in this little box is a set of blue dishes."

"I will take them," said Hans and home he ran and dropped them in Gretchen's stocking. Then he went to bed.

Early in the morning the children came running downstairs.

"Oh!" said Gretchen, "look at my stocking," and when she saw the blue dishes she was as happy as could be, but Peterkin could never understand how his candy heart changed into a box of blue dishes. Can you?

Author untraced

THE POPPY-SEED CAKES

ONCE upon a time there was a little boy and his name was Andrewshek. His mother and his father brought him from the old country when he was a tiny baby.

Andrewshek had an Auntie Katushka and she came from the old country, too, on Andrewshek's fourth birthday.

Andrewshek's Auntie Katushka came on a large boat. She brought with her a huge bag filled with presents for Andrewshek and his father and his mother. In the huge bag were a fine feather bed and a bright shawl and five pounds of poppy seeds.

The fine feather bed was made from the feathers of her old green goose at home. It was to keep Andrewshek warm when he took a nap.

The bright shawl was for Andrewshek's Auntie Katushka to wear when she went to market.

The five pounds of poppy seeds were to sprinkle on little cakes which Andrewshek's Auntie Katushka made every Saturday for Andrewshek.

One lovely Saturday morning Andrewshek's Auntie Katushka took some butter and some sugar and some flour and some milk and seven eggs and she rolled out some nice little cakes. Then she sprinkled each cake with some of the poppy seeds which she had brought from the old country.

While the nice little cakes were baking, she spread out the fine feather bed on top of the big bed for Andrewshek to take his nap. Andrewshek did not like to take a nap.

Andrewshek loved to bounce up and down and up and down on his fine feather bed.

Andrewshek's Auntie Katushka took the nice little cakes out of the oven and put them on the table to cool; then she put on her bright shawl to go to market.

"Andrewshek," she said, "please watch these cakes while you rest on your fine feather bed. Be sure that the kitten and the dog do not go near them."

"Yes, indeed! I will watch the nice little cakes," said Andrewshek. "And I will be sure that the kitten and the dog do not touch them." But all Andrewshek really did was to bounce up and down and up and down on the fine feather bed.

"Andrewshek!" said Andrewshek's Auntie Katushka, "how can you watch the poppy-seed cakes when all you do is to bounce up and down and up and down on the fine feather bed?" Then Andrewshek's Auntie Katushka, in her bright shawl, hurried off to market.

But Andrewshek kept bouncing up and down and up and down on the fine feather bed and paid no attention to the little cakes sprinkled with poppy seeds.

Just as Andrewshek was bouncing up in the air for the ninth time, he heard a queer noise that sounded like "Hs-s-s-s-sss," at the front door of his house.

"Oh, what a queer noise!" cried Andrewshek. He jumped down off the fine feather bed and opened the front door. There stood a great green goose as big as Andrewshek himself. The goose was very cross and was scolding as fast as he could. He was wagging his head and was opening and closing his long red beak.

"What do you want?" said Andrewshek. "What are you scolding about?"

"I want all the goose feathers from your fine feather bed," quacked the big green goose. "They are mine."

"They are not yours," said Andrewshek. "My Auntie Katushka brought them with her from the old country in a huge bag."

"They are mine," quacked the big green goose. He waddled over to the fine feather bed and tugged at it with his long red beak.

"Stop, Green Goose!" said Andrewshek, "and I will give you one of Auntie Katushka's poppy-seed cakes."

"A poppy-seed cake!" the green goose quacked in delight. "I love nice little poppy-seed cakes! Give me one and you shall have your feather bed."

But one poppy-seed cake could not satisfy the greedy green goose.

"Give me another!" Andrewshek gave the green goose another poppy-seed cake.

"Give me another!" the big green goose hissed and frightened Andrewshek nearly out of his wits.

Andrewshek gave him another and another and another till all the poppy-seed cakes were gone.

Just as the last poppy-seed cake disappeared down the long neck of the green goose, Andrewshek's Auntie Katushka appeared at the door, in her bright shawl. "Boo! hoo!" cried Andrewshek. "See! that naughty green goose has eaten all the poppy-seed cakes."

"What? All my nice little poppy-seed cakes?" cried Andrewshek's Auntie Katushka. "The naughty goose!"

The greedy goose tugged at the fine feather bed again with his long red beak and started to drag it to the door. Andrewshek's Auntie Katushka ran after the green goose and just then there was a dreadful explosion. The greedy goose who had stuffed himself with poppy-seed cakes had burst and his feathers flew all over the room.

"Well! well!" said Andrewshek's Auntie Katushka, as she gathered up the pieces of the big green goose. "We soon shall have two fine feather pillows for your fine feather bed."

By Margery Clark

THE PICNIC BASKET

ONE cool summer morning Andrewshek's Auntie Katushka said, "Andrewshek, I think I will put some sandwiches and some cottage cheese and some poppy-seed cakes and two eggs in our picnic basket. Then we will go to the park and eat our lunch there, near the water."

"May I go with you, Auntie Katushka?" said Andrewshek.

"Of course you may go to the park with me," said Auntie Katushka. "But first we have a great many things to do, before we can start to the park. I must go into the garden and catch the white goat. I will tie her up so she will not run away. Please find the kitten, Andrewshek, and put her in the cellar, so she will not worry the chickens while we are gone."

But all Andrewshek really did was to lift up the red and white napkin which Auntie Katushka had laid over the picnic basket and look at the eggs and the poppy-seed cakes and touch the sandwiches and taste the cottage cheese.

The goat was not easy to catch. The goat wanted to go to the park, too. She galloped round and round the garden.

At last Auntie Katushka caught her and tied her firmly to a post.

Then Auntie Katushka went into the house to get Andrewshek and the lunch basket. She saw Andrewshek peeping under the red and white napkin and tasting the cottage cheese. He had forgotten all about the kitten.

The kitten was nowhere to be found. "I think she must be paying a visit to the mouse family," said Auntie Katushka.

Then Auntie Katushka put on her bright shawl and took her umbrella with the long crooked handle under

one arm. Then she picked up the lunch basket with the red and white napkin on top and she and Andrewshek started for the park.

They went down the hill and across the tracks and past the market and down a long street until they came to the park by the water.

Andrewshek sat down on the grass beside a little stream. Andrewshek's Auntie Katushka laid her umbrella with the long crooked handle and the basket of lunch on the grass beside Andrewshek.

"Andrewshek," said Auntie Katushka, "I must go to the spring and get some water for us to drink. Please watch the basket with the eggs and the sandwiches and poppy-seed cakes and cottage cheese while I am gone."

"Yes, indeed, I will watch the basket of lunch," said Andrewshek.

But what Andrewshek really did was to say to himself, "I would like to take off my shoes and my stockings and wade in the little stream. I believe I will!"

Andrewshek took off his shoes and his stockings and went wading in the little stream.

A big white swan came floating calmly down the stream. He saw the picnic basket lying on the grass. He stopped and stretched and stretched his long neck, till he could touch the basket. "Honk! honk! honk!" said he. "I wonder what is under the red and white napkin."

The big white swan lifted the napkin with his red bill and looked in the basket. "Oh, oh, oh! Won't Mother Swan be pleased with this nice lunch!" said he. "Sandwich bread makes fine food for baby swans."

He picked up the basket in his strong red bill and floated it ahead of him down the stream.

Andrewshek could not wade after the big white swan. The water was too deep.

"Stop! stop! White Swan!" cried Andrewshek. "That is my Auntie Katushka's picnic basket and it has our lunch in it. Please put it back on the grass."

"No, indeed! I will not put the basket back," honked the big white swan. "Sandwich bread makes fine food for baby swans and I have ten baby swans to feed."

The big white swan gave the picnic basket a little push with his red bill. The basket floated on down the little stream. The big white swan floated calmly behind it.

Just then Andrewshek's Auntie Katushka came hurrying up with the spring water. She saw the big white swan floating down the stream, with the lunch basket floating ahead of him.

Andrewshek stood in the middle of the stream, crying.

Auntie Katushka picked up her umbrella with the long crooked handle. Auntie Katushka ran along the shore until she overtook the big white swan, with the lunch basket floating ahead of him.

She caught the handle of the picnic basket in the crook of her long-handled umbrella. She drew the basket safely to shore.

"Well! well!" said Auntie Katushka, as she spread the red and white napkin on the grass, and laid the sandwiches and the poppy-seed cakes and the cottage cheese and the eggs upon it. "It always pays to carry an umbrella to a picnic."

By Margery Clark

THE TEA PARTY

THE next morning Andrewshek's Auntie Katushka said to Andrewshek, "I think I will make some poppy-seed cakes."

Then she took some butter and some sugar and some flour and some milk and nine eggs and rolled out some nice little cakes.

"Why are you making so many nice little poppy-seed cakes?" asked Andrewshek.

"Because we are going to have a tea party this afternoon," said Auntie Katushka. She sprinkled each little cake with some of the poppy seeds she had brought from the old country.

"Who is coming to the tea party?" asked Andrewshek, as he watched his Auntie Katushka put the poppy-seed cakes in the oven.

"Erminka and Erminka's mother and Erminka's little brother," said Auntie Katushka.

"Oh, goody!" said Andrewshek. "And I hope Erminka brings her wooden dolls."

Andrewshek's Auntie Katushka took off her kitchen apron and hung it on a nail beside the door. She took the nice little cakes out of the oven and put them on the table to cool. Then she went to the cupboard drawer and took out her very best silk apron and the bright shawl which she had brought from the old country. She laid the apron and the shawl on the fine feather bed.

"When it is time for the tea party, I will put these on," said Auntie Katushka to Andrewshek. "Now I am going next door to invite Erminka and Erminka's mother and Erminka's little brother to the tea party.

Please watch the kitchen door while I am gone. Be sure that the kitten and the dog and the chickens do not come into the house."

"Yes, indeed! I will watch the kitchen door while you are gone next door," said Andrewshek. "And I will be sure that the kitten and the dog and the chickens do not come into the house."

But all Andrewshek really did was to put on Auntie Katushka's very best silk apron and her bright shawl and walk back and forth and back and forth in front of the mirror. He paid no attention to the kitchen door.

Just as Andrewshek was walking back and forth and back and forth in front of the mirror for the eleventh time, he heard a great commotion at the kitchen door. The kitten and the dog and the two chickens and the white goat had come into the kitchen.

They went straight to the kitchen table.

"Don't I see poppy-seed cakes?" the white goat asked Andrewshek.

"They smell delicious!" said the kitten and the dog and the two chickens.

"Auntie Katushka made the poppy-seed cakes for a tea party," said Andrewshek.

"Are we invited to the tea party?" asked the white goat.

"Are we invited to the tea party?" asked the kitten and the dog and the two chickens.

"I think not," said Andrewshek. "Here comes Auntie Katushka, I will ask her."

The kitten and the dog and the two chickens and the white goat ran out of the door and into the garden as fast as they could go. Andrewshek took off the best silk

— 67 —

apron and the bright shawl and laid them on the fine feather bed.

"Erminka and Erminka's mother and Erminka's little brother will come to our tea party at exactly half-past three," said Andrewshek's Auntie Katushka.

At exactly half-past three Erminka and Erminka's mother and Erminka's little brother came to the tea party.

Erminka brought her wooden dolls. Erminka wore her new black slippers.

Erminka and Andrewshek and Erminka's little brother played together with Erminka's dolls around the corner of the house, near the front gate. Erminka said, "My mother says we may have a tea party for you and your Auntie Katushka at my house tomorrow and have gooseberry tarts."

"Goody!" said Andrewshek.

Andrewshek's Auntie Katushka spread a clean white tablecloth on the table under the apple tree in the garden. She brought out two plates of poppy-seed cakes and five cups and saucers and five spoons and five napkins. Then she went back into the house to get some strawberry jam.

The white goat and the kitten and the dog and the two chickens came and sat down on the bench beside the table under the apple tree in the garden. They sat very quiet with their hands folded.

"If we behave nicely," said the white goat, "perhaps Andrewshek's Auntie Katushka will let us join the tea party."

Andrewshek's Auntie Katushka came out on the porch with a bowl of strawberry jam in her hand. She saw the white goat and the kitten and the dog and the two chickens sitting quiet on the bench, with their hands folded.

"Well! well!" said Auntie Katushka. "Some more friends have come to our tea party. I hope they will like poppy-seed cakes and strawberry jam, too."

And they did.

By Margery Clark

THE JACK-O'-LANTERN

OVER in Cherry Valley lives a boy named Peter. Peter has a wagon, a little red wagon.

One bright day in autumn, when the leaves were all scarlet and yellow, and clusters of bittersweet berries showed orange along the wayside, Peter went up the road with his little red wagon.

Up, up he went till he came to a cornfield where pumpkins were growing. Peter turned at the gateway and went into the field; for he wanted to make a jack-o'-lantern, and he was after a pumpkin.

Pumpkins, pumpkins everywhere! The field was dotted with them—big and little, green and yellow.

Peter passed them by one after another. This one was too light; that one, too dark; the next, too large; the next, too small. Then he came to a flat one. He didn't want that.

But after a while Peter stopped. Before him was a pumpkin the color of gold, not too little, and not too big—just right for a jack-o'-lantern.

"Oh-ho!" cried Peter. "Mister Pum-pumpkin, you're going to home with me. You're going to have

"Big eyes to see
And teeth to bite;
So I can have fun
On Hallowe'en night."

It took some tugging, but at last Peter got the pumpkin into his wagon. Then down the road he came running like a runaway horse.

The wagon went bump, bump, bump!

The pumpkin went jump, jump, jump!

Peter was galloping along, when all of a sudden the wagon ran bang! against a big stone and upset. Away rolled the pumpkin down a steep, rocky hill. Over and over and over it tumbled until it struck a tree. Then—plop! It flew into pieces!

Peter said, "I *must* have a pumpkin: I want to make a jack-o'-lantern

"With eyes to see
And teeth to bite;
So I can have fun
On Hallowe'en night."

— 70 —

And up the road he went again with his little red wagon.

Peter found another pumpkin the color of gold, not too little, and not too big. He tugged till he got it into his wagon. Then down the road he came running as fast as before.

The wagon went bump, bump, bump,
The pumpkin went jump, jump, jump!

Peter was clip-clapping along when, in a field at the side of the road, he spied the ears of a rabbit sticking up in a patch of clover. To see the rabbit better, Peter left the wagon and climbed over the wall. When he came back, a cow was eating his pumpkin! The big white seeds lay scattered all over the ground.

Peter said, "I *must* have a pumpkin: I want to make a jack-o'-lantern

> "With eyes to see
> And teeth to bite;
> So I can have fun
> On Hallowe'en night."

And up the road he went again with his little red wagon.

Peter found another pumpkin the color of gold, not too little, and not too big. He tugged till he got it into his wagon. Then down the road he came running as fast as ever.

> The wagon went bump, bump, bump!
> The pumpkin went jump, jump, jump!

Peter ran past the big stone, clippity-clap. He passed the cow. He passed the field where the rabbit was eating.

Farther on a squirrel sat on the wall with its tail curled up its back and a nut in its paws. Peter saw it, but he didn't stop. He wouldn't stop for anything—anything at all, but ran on and on till he was at home.

"Ha!" said Peter, "now I'll make a jack-o'-lantern —a funny one." Then he looked in his wagon. No pumpkin there! Peter had lost the pumpkin. It had jumped out of the wagon.

Peter said, "I *must* have a pumpkin: I want to make a jack-o'-lantern

> "With eyes to see
> And teeth to bite;
> So I can have fun
> On Hallowe'en night."

"Polly! Polly!" Peter called to his sister. "Will you

go up to the cornfield? I want you to help me get a pumpkin."

Polly was willing; so up the road they both went with the little red wagon.

They found a pumpkin the color of gold, not too little, and not too big. They boosted it into the wagon. Then down the road they came walking—cl-ap, cl-ap. All the way home they walked very slowly, with Polly behind holding on to the pumpkin.

The wagon didn't bump, bump, bump!

The pumpkin didn't jump, jump, jump!

It jogged along merrily over hummocks and stones, and right up to the doorstep in Peter's back yard.

Then Peter made a jack-o'-lantern.

He cut two eyes and a three-cornered nose, and a mouth big enough to take in a whole pie at a bite.

The jack-o'-lantern stood on a porch post with a red candle inside. Its eyes, round as cart wheels, glowed like fire in the dark; and its mouth showed rows of long, sharp teeth.

The cat was so frightened she ran under the porch.
Little Dog Jack backed away and barked and barked.

"Polly!" called Peter. "Polly, come out! My jack-o'-
lantern

"Has eyes to see
And teeth to bite.
Come and have fun;
It's Hallowe'en night."

By Mabel G. La Rue

A VISIT TO THE FARM

Look at the turkey gobbler.
  Oh, see him strut along,
His tail spread out into a fan.
  Just listen to his song:
    "Gobble, gobble, gobble,
      Gobble, gobble, gob."

Look at the geese a-waddling,
  A-waddling as they walk,
Their necks stretched forward as they go.
  And this is how they talk:
    "Honk-honk-honk,
      Honk-honk, honk-honk."

Look at the rooster stretching up.
He stands so proudly tall.
His wings they flap, his comb shows red.
Now, listen to his call:
"Cockadoodle, cockadoodle,
Cockadoodle-doo."

Look at the ducks go gliding
Into the water clear.
As they swim out across the pond
Their language you can hear:
"Quack, quack, quack,
Quack-quack, quack-quack."

And so, you see, each feathered friend
Speaks in a different way.
"Gobble, cockadoodle-doo,
Honk-honk, and quack," they say.

Once a little girl went to spend a day at a farm in the country. The farm belonged to Uncle Ned. The little girl's name was Betty Anne. Uncle Ned offered to take Betty Anne around the farm to see all the animals.

In one field were some cows—some black and white cows. They were chewing hay and looking lazily around. One black and white cow had a tiny baby black and white . . . calf. As Betty Anne stood there watching, the cows began to moo. They lifted their heads. It seemed to Betty Anne that they were saying:
"Moo, moo, moo,
We give our milk to you."

In the next field were some horses. There was a chestnut-brown horse, there was a snow-white horse, there was a dapple-gray horse, and there was a black horse with a tiny baby . . . colt. And there was a black and white pony, too. When the pony saw Betty Anne, he ran over to the fence whinnying. It seemed to Betty Anne that he was saying:

"Wheeee, wheeee,
Come ride on me."

Next door in another field were some sheep, with woolly fur all over them. There was a mother sheep with a little tiny baby . . . lamb. The mother said, "Bah, ha, ha," and the baby answered, "Maa-aa-aa."

There were some pigs, too. They were big and grunty. There was one enormous fat pig with three baby piggiewigs. She kept saying, "Wunk, wunk, wunk," to them in a low gruff voice, and they kept squealing back at her in tiny weeny voices. It seemed to Betty Anne that they were saying:

"Ooee, ooee, ooee, say we,
Little baby piggies three."

Betty Anne and Uncle Ned came to some bunnies next. They were soft and cuddly looking and had long, long ears, and they didn't say anything at all. They just went hop, hop, hop, and jump, jump, jump, and then sat still and wiggled their noses, and ate carrots and lettuce and cabbage.

The chicken yard was way at the far end of the farm. Uncle Ned showed Betty Anne how the pigeons flew about in a pen covered with wire meshing. The pigeons looked at Betty Anne with unblinky eyes. They seemed to be saying:

"Coo, coorooroo,
And how are you?"

Uncle Ned showed Betty Anne the chickens, too. He showed her how the nests in which the hens laid their eggs were arranged like little boxes in the wall. The hens would fly up into the nests, which had straw in the bottom. Whenever one of the hens laid an egg she would get very excited. Then she would sound as if she were calling out:

"Cuck-cuck-cuck-cuck-caw-awk,
I've laid an egg for you,
Cuck-cawk and now I'm through."

Uncle Ned showed Betty Anne a mother hen with some little yellow baby chicks. The mother hen kept calling, "Cluck, cluck, cluck," to the baby chicks, and they kept answering, "Eep, eep, eep," as if they were asking:

"Tweet, weet, weet,
Aren't we sweet?"

And the big rooster, who didn't want to be forgotten, crowed as loudly as he could, as if he were saying:

"Cock-a-doodle-doo,
Look at me, too."

Then what do you think Betty Anne saw standing way over in the corner with a tail spread out behind like a fan? A turkey gobbler, a real live Thanksgiving turkey. He just stood there without saying anything at all.

"Doesn't he talk?" asked Betty Anne.

"Oh yes, he does," answered Uncle Ned. "He says, 'Gobble, gobble, gobble.' I imagine when he says 'Gobble-gobble' that he's trying to sing

" 'On Thanksgiving day you'll see
You will want to gobble me.' "

And Uncle Ned grinned.

"It's starting to grow dark, Betty," he continued, "so I guess we had better be getting back to the house."

On the way back they called good-by to the turkey, who said . . . "Gobble-gobble"; and to the rooster, who said . . . "Cock-a-doodle-doo"; and to the hen, who said . . . "Cuck-cuck, cuck-cuck-cawk"; and to the baby chicks, who said . . . "Eep, eep, eep"; and to the pigeons, who said . . . "Cooroo, coorooo"; and to the piggies, who said . . . "Ooee, ooee, ooee"; and to the pony that called . . . "Whee-ee-ee"; and to the cow who said . . . "Moo, moo, moo"; and to the lamb, who said . . . "Maa-aa-aa"; and to the bunnies that didn't say anything at all but just went hop, hop, hop, and jump, jump, jump.

> So many animals we've seen,
> It's been a lovely day!
> And each and every one of them
> Had something else to say,
> And each and every one of them
> Spoke in a different way.
>
> *By Dorothy Baruch*

(Dots in this story indicate a pause while listeners think of and supply the word.)

WEE ANN SPENDS A PENNY

WEE ANN was sewing. She was making a patchwork quilt for Mary Queen of Scots' bed. Grandmother had showed her how to sew the little squares, and she had put four pieces together that very morning. One was a square of black silk with a violet stripe—that was a bit of Grandmother's Sunday dress. Then came a piece of lovely blue—Aunt Jean's summer suit.

"Now something of Uncle Jamie's, please," asked Wee Ann.

So Grandmother gave her an old green necktie that just suited Wee Ann's taste. Aunt Jean hunted up a box of ribbons which she said Wee Ann might have, and from it Wee Ann chose next a square of pale pink that fitted in nicely beside the bright green.

Wee Ann and Aunt Jean were sitting out on the piazza. It was cool and shady, and now and then a little breeze blew Wee Ann's curls in her eyes, and made her scraps of silk fly up in the air like so many gay-colored butterflies. Wee Ann could smell the lilac bush down by the gate, and she liked to watch the robins who made themselves very much at home under Grandmother MacKenzie's trees.

It was pleasant there, and Wee Ann was glad she had come visiting.

Wee Ann sat sewing and Aunt Jean was writing a letter—that is, she was trying to write a letter, but Wee Ann was so sociable this morning, there were so many things to talk about, that Aunt Jean found letter writing hard work.

"Would you put yellow next, on this piece with the cunning little red spots, Aunt Jean?" asked Wee Ann.

"The yellow, I think," said Aunt Jean, crossing out a word in her letter.

"Please make a knot, Aunt Jean."

"Aunt Jean, have those robins a nest in one of our trees, do you think?"

"It wouldn't surprise me," answered Aunt Jean, crossing another word.

"Which tree do you think it is, Aunt Jean?"

"Um-um," said Auntie.

"I said which tree do you think it is, Aunt Jean?"

"Wee Ann," said Aunt Jean, "I'm going in the house to finish my letter. I think I can write better at the desk."

"I'll go in with you, Auntie," said her niece. "The wind blows my silk away."

Aunt Jean laughed. "I'll tell you what I'll do, Wee
Ann," said she; "I'll give you a penny, and you go up
street to Mrs. Hopp's, and buy whatever you like."

"Oh, Aunt Jean, Aunt Jean!" cried Wee Ann, tumbling the patchwork quilt into her sewing box; "how
good you are!"

She threw her arms round Aunt Jean's neck and
"rubbed cheeks" affectionately.

"I'll hurry right back!"

Aunt Jean laughed again. "Don't walk too fast," said
she—"the sun is hot."

So Wee Ann started off up the street to spend her
penny.

She thought over all the things she might buy with
it. A tiny doll for Mary Queen of Scots, a licorice shoe
string, a little balloon with a whistle (Wee Ann called
it a "squeaker"), chewing gum—no, Wee Ann knew
Aunt Jean wouldn't want her penny spent for chewing
gum. Perhaps she would buy a present for Aunt Jean,
or something for Uncle Jamie, but then it would be too
bad to leave Grandmother out.

"I'll look and look a long time before I spend my
penny," thought Wee Ann.

Mrs. Hopp's store was in the front room of her own
little house. It had one big window, and in the window
were boxes of writing paper and pads, pencils and bot-
tles of ink. Inside on the shelves were boxes that held
needles and pins and spools of thread. There were jars
of candy, too, lemon sticks, thick pieces of black licorice, pink and white striped peppermint candy. In a
case were packages of tobacco, pipes—fancy brown
ones and white ones, too—and more candy in glass

dishes, and this was where Wee Ann meant to look before she made her choice.

Wee Ann knew just where the shop was. First the church, then the minister's house, then the little cottage where the dressmaker lived. You knew this house by the gay-colored fashion plates, that would make such good paper dolls, pinned in the window, and next to this came the shop.

Wee Ann knew Mrs. Hopp, too. She was little and thin and always wore her spectacles pushed up on her forehead. Wee Ann wondered how she could see with them there. She was patient, and would let you take as long as you liked to make up your mind.

So Wee Ann tripped up street, past the church, past the minister's house, past the dressmaker's, and in at the shop door.

But no Mrs. Hopp was to be seen. A big man in farmer's overalls and a flapping straw hat stood behind the counter talking to a woman who had a pail on her arm and held in her hand a paper of pins she had just bought.

"Yes, Mrs. Hopp she went in a hurry," said the man. He was Mr. Hopp, but Wee Ann didn't know this. "She didn't even have time to lock up. Yes, I guess her daughter's real sick. I'm going to shut shop now. I have to work in the garden."

The woman went out, and Mr. Hopp reached down a big key that hung behind the door.

Wee Ann stood on tiptoe and peered hurriedly into the case. First came the packages of tobacco, next the pipes, and then she saw a glass dish of pink and white candy bananas.

"Well, little gel," boomed Mr. Hopp's big voice.

Wee Ann pointed to the candy bananas.

"A white one, please," she said.

She laid down her penny, took the bag Mr. Hopp handed her, and darted out of the store.

She ran a little way, for she wanted to get home. It had been so different from what she had expected. But at the church steps she sat down. She would take a peep at her candy banana. Surely it was big enough to share with Aunt Jean, and Uncle Jamie, and Grandmother.

Wee Ann opened her bag. Then her eyes grew big and round and her face puckered up as if she was going to cry. For what do you think she saw inside the paper bag? A pipe! A white clay pipe that Mr. Hopp had given her by mistake.

Wee Ann picked up her paper bag and started home. Tears rolled down her cheeks as she ran, and by the time she reached her own gate she was crying out loud, yes, and making just as much noise as Tommy Nelson in the railway station.

Aunt Jean had finished her letter and she came running out on the piazza.

She held out her arms, and Wee Ann came sobbing up the walk and fell into them.

"I spent my penny," she sobbed, "I bought a banana, a white candy banana, and the man didn't give it to me. He's locked the store and Mrs. Hopp has gone away and he didn't give me my banana."

"What did he give you?" asked Aunt Jean. "What is in that bag?"

"A pipe!" answered Wee Ann with a sniff. "He gave me a pipe."

Aunt Jean wanted to laugh, it was so funny to think of little Wee Ann with a pipe. But she didn't even smile.

"Let us look at it," said she.

But when she opened the paper bag and took out the little clay pipe, then Aunt Jean did laugh.

"Why, Wee Ann," said she, "don't you know what to do with this pipe? It's much better than a candy banana, I'm sure. Come and I'll show you." And Aunt Jean led the way into the house.

First she filled a bowl with water and into it she put a cake of soap. Wee Ann didn't know what to make of it.

"Now," said Aunt Jean briskly, "stir that soap around until the water is just as soapy as it can be. I'll be back in a minute."

And in a minute back she came with a little bottle, and she poured something from it into the soapy water.

"Oh, what is it, Aunt Jean?" asked Wee Ann. Her face was streaked with tears and her nose was red, but she had forgotten to cry.

"Glycerine," said Aunt Jean. "Good for chapped hands and for soap bubbles too." And Aunt Jean dipped the pipe into the water and blew the most beautiful bubble you ever saw. It was pink and green and blue and violet and every other pretty color you can imagine.

"Let me, let me!" cried Wee Ann, hopping up and down. So Wee Ann blew another beautiful bubble while the first one floated about the room.

"It would be nice on the piazza," said Wee Ann.

So Aunt Jean carried the bowl out on the piazza and there Wee Ann blew bubbles all the morning.

"Wouldn't you rather have this than a candy banana?" asked Aunt Jean.

"Oh, yes, indeed! I'm just as glad as I can be that I bought this soap-bubble pipe," answered Wee Ann with a smile.

By Ethel Calvert Phillips

A CITY STREET

GREEN light!
  Come along! What are you waiting for? Honk, honk!
  The procession moves.

  Autos, taxis, busses, trucks move along, jammed so
  close they almost touch. Autos, taxis, busses, trucks,
  autos, taxis, busses, trucks, autos, taxis . . .

  Honk, honk, who blocks the way?
  Honk, honk, are you deaf? hey!
  Honk, honk, Honk! Honk! Honk! Honk!
  That moving van will take all day!

  Autos, taxis, busses, trucks,
  Autos, taxis, busses, trucks!

  The procession moves down the city street.

Red light!
  The procession freezes.

  Now the cross-town traffic moves.
  Autos, and trucks, autos, and trucks.

  Dash to the sidewalk, dash to the policeman,
  Look sharp, look sharp!

  Autos and trucks, autos and trucks,
  Autos and trucks, autos and trucks!

  The cross-town traffic moves across the street.

Green light!
  The procession moves.

Red light!
  The procession freezes.

Green light!
Red light!
Green light!
Red light!

  The procession moves and freezes,
  moves and freezes on the city street.
                              By Lucy Sprague Mitchell

CHARLIE RIDES IN THE ENGINE OF A REAL TRAIN

ONE day Charlie and his mother and his auntie and Topsy and Bingo and Jane went to stay in the country.

It was a very interesting place where they were going to stay in the country. What do you think? It was the place where Charlie's daddy had lived when he was a little boy!

Yes, that is where they were going, and, as it was a Saturday, Charlie's daddy was going with them too. He was not going to live with them in the country, because on week days he had to go to the office every day. But he said that he would come down *every* Saturday and stay in the country till Sunday night.

So they all went to the railway station in a taxicab. Jane traveled in a cat basket and Charlie's auntie carried her. Topsy also traveled in a cat basket and Charlie's mother carried him, but Bingo had to travel in the baggage car and he had a ticket all to himself because he was a dog. Charlie thought that he ought to feel very proud.

When they got to the station they all went straight through the gate to the platform, and there the train was waiting for them. It was a great enormous train with ever so many coaches. First, Charlie and his daddy took Bingo to the baggage car, and the baggage man fastened Bingo's leash to the end of a trunk and promised Charlie to be good to Bingo.

Then they all got into the day car, and the train gave a loud whistle and steamed out of the station. My goodness! how fast it went! Everything just seemed to go flying past.

Soon the conductor came walking down the aisle and he took everybody's ticket. He was a very grand-looking man; he was tall, and stout, and he had a beautiful blue uniform on. He soon came to the seat where Charlie and his daddy were sitting, and he took the tickets. Yes, the conductor took all the tickets and he stuck Charlie's daddy's ticket in his hatband, but as his mother and his auntie had no hatbands, he stuck *their* tickets into the top of the seat in front of them. Then he took Charlie's ticket, and he stuck it in Charlie's hatband. Charlie felt very proud, and he would not take his hat off. No, he kept his hat on all the time because he wanted everybody to see that *he* had a ticket in his hatband just like all the other men.

Then Charlie said to his daddy, "Daddy, what exactly makes the train go?"

And his daddy said, "It's the steam that makes the engine work, and it is the engineer and the fireman who look after the steam and the engine."

Then Charlie said, "What I want to know is exactly what the fireman and the engineer do when they are making the engine go."

But what do you think? His daddy did not know exactly what they did—he said that he had never ridden on an engine in his life, so how could he know what they did? And Charlie's mother and his auntie did not know either. That was very surprising.

Well, after they had been in the big train for about a whole hour, they came to a station where there were a lot of tracks. This station was called a junction, because there were so many tracks.

Some of the tracks went to the North and some to the South and some to the East and some to the West. The train that Charlie and his daddy and his auntie and his mother were on was going toward the West; but now they wanted to go to the North, so they had to change trains and go on a train that was going toward the North.

The train was already waiting on its own track. It was a very little train, it had only two coaches!

Charlie's mother and his auntie and Jane and Topsy got into the train, and they took Bingo with them, because, as it was such a little unimportant train, the conductor said that Bingo could travel in the day coach instead of being tied up in the baggage car, and Bingo was very glad. But Charlie and his daddy waited on the platform till it was time for the train to start, and they looked at all the interesting things about them.

Then a man came up. He wore overalls and a peaked cap. And—you never can guess who it was! It was the fireman who helped work the engine of the train they were going to take. And what do you think? The fireman knew Charlie's daddy! Yes, the fireman came up to them, and said to his daddy, "Hello, Bob!" Bob was his daddy's name that his mother and his auntie always called him! And his daddy said, "Why, hello, Bill," and they shook hands.

Charlie was very much surprised that the fireman and his daddy knew each other, but it was not so very surprising after all. The fireman lived in the village where Charlie's daddy had lived when he was a little boy, and where Charlie and his mother and his auntie were going to live for a whole month, and his daddy and the fireman had gone to the same school when they were little boys!

Well, the fireman then looked at Charlie, and he said, "And is this your boy?"

Then Charlie's daddy said, "Yes, this is Charlie, and you are the very man he wants to meet. Charlie wants to know exactly what the fireman and the engineer do to make the train go—and he can't find anybody who knows. So go ahead and tell him all about it."

But the fireman said, "I can do better than that. Suppose you and Charlie take a ride on the engine with

me; then he can see everything with his own eyes, and learn all there is to know in case he wants to be a fireman himself."

Yes, the fireman actually said those words! And Charlie's daddy said, "That will be fine. I'll just go and tell Charlie's mother and his auntie what has become of us, so they won't worry."

And he did so. Then the fireman, and Charlie and his daddy all got into the cab, which is back of the engine, where the engineer and the fireman sit.

The engineer was already sitting in his place, which is on the right of the cab. He was very pleased to meet Charlie and his daddy, but he said that after the train had started he would not be able to speak a word to anybody, and nobody must speak to him. Yes, nobody must ever speak to the engineer when he is driving the engine, because if anybody spoke to the engineer it might distract his attention and then the train might be wrecked!

All the time that the train is going the engineer has to sit on his seat with his hand on the throttle, which is the thing that makes the train stop in a hurry, and all the time he has to look out of the window to see what the signals say, and to see that there is nothing on the track ahead of him.

If he sees a green signal on the signal post that means that the engine can go straight ahead, but if the signal is red, then it means "Stop"—and the engineer presses on the throttle, and the train stops.

The engineer told all this to Charlie while they were waiting for the train to start. Then the engineer got the signal from the man on the platform; he blew the whistle, and the train started, and he could not say another word.

Well, the fireman's place is on the left side of the cab, and Charlie's daddy sat between him and the window, and Charlie sat on his daddy's knee.

The fireman has to work very hard, but when he is not working he can talk if he wants to. This fireman was very kind and, when he was not working, he explained everything to Charlie and his daddy—but all the time he was explaining he had to keep looking out of the window, too, in case he should see anything that the engineer did not see. There are a great many windows in the cab of an engine—it has windows all round, because it is so very important that the engineer and the fireman shall see all that there is to see.

Well, I will now tell you what the fireman was doing all the time that Charlie and his daddy were riding on the engine with him.

In front of the fireman was the steam gauge, which is a round thing like a clock, and it has a hand like a clock hand, too, and the steam makes the hand move— so that you can see how much steam is coming out of the boiler. When the steam is getting low the hand drops, and when the hand of the gauge drops to one hundred and fifty the fireman knows it is time to put more coal in the fire box.

Every time that the hand of the gauge dropped to one hundred and fifty the fireman got up and opened a little door in the back of the cab, which opened right into the fire box, so that you could see the fire all red and glowing, and the fireman scooped a great shovelful of coal into it. The fireman told Charlie that it was very important how one shovels the coal into the fire box. It has to be shoveled very evenly, so that it is not all black with coal in one place and all red hot with embers in another place. Yes, the fireman told Charlie that it needs a lot of practice before one can shovel the coal in just exactly right.

Then the fireman also had to watch the water gauge, which shows how much water there is in the boiler.

When he saw by the water gauge that the water was getting low in the boiler, then the fireman had to turn a valve, which is a sort of handle that starts a pump working, and the pump pumps water into the boiler.

Charlie very much wanted to turn the valve himself, but the fireman said No, that it needed a whole lot of practice before one could pump water into the tank— as it was very important just how much water to pump. If too much cold water is pumped into the boiler it might cool the water already in the boiler so that no more steam would come out—and then the train would stop!

Do you think that the fireman on an engine is a busy man? Indeed he is!

But that is not all that the fireman has to do. Oh, dear, no! The fireman has a lot more work to do.

When the train is coming to a steep place—and there were a lot of steep places on the railroad that Charlie was traveling on—the fireman has to make the fire *red hot,* so that lots and lots of steam can come out of the boiler. He makes the fire get hotter and hotter until the steam gets so strong that the "safety valve" pops off— and this shows the engineer that there is enough steam to push the train up the steep place. Yes, you can see that it would need a lot of extra steam to push a train up a steep, high hill.

The fireman also has to blow a whistle, whenever the train comes to a crossing or to the station. And when they got to the last stop—which was the village where Charlie and his mother and his auntie and Bingo and Topsy and Jane were going to live for a whole month —the fireman let Charlie blow the whistle himself! Yes, he did, and you should have heard what a loud whistle Charlie blew.

Well, at last they had come to the end of their journey, and Charlie certainly had learned a whole lot about engines. Yes, Charlie had learned a whole lot more than most people know. Of course he told his mother and his auntie about everything, so that they, too, should know all about what the fireman and the engineer do to make the train go.

And Charlie said, "Now, when I get home to the city I will be able to play with my train in just the right way. I will be able to play that I am the fireman and the engineer, and I will know exactly what they do, and I will practice and practice being a fireman so that I can be one when I grow up!"

By Helen Hill and Violet Maxwell

THE PONY WITH A PAST

THERE were once five little children who spent a lot of time teasing for a pony. Their hearts beat as one, they were filled with but a single desire; they thought, chattered, and dreamed of nothing but pony; all five together wished one huge wish continually, till finally and fortunately somebody had a birthday and a pony appeared at the door.

The pony resembled closely vanilla ice cream with hot chocolate sauce and was in fact so attractive looking that they named him Sundae. After much shrill delight, Sundae was hitched to a charming pony cart like a flower basket and all five little children, whose names do not matter here, clambered in and prepared for the lovely drive to which they had looked forward so long. The gentle governess took up the reins and shook them mildly, the children bounced up and down like a fluttering bouquet and made clucking sounds to indicate their readiness to start, the stable boy stood by and called "Giddap!" with vehemence; but nothing happened. It was then perceived by all that, despite his beauty, Sundae was not an agreeable character, nor in any way amenable to the wishes of the five little children whose pleasure he was intended to promote. On the contrary, he would not move from the spot.

What could they do? True, there was a pretty whip; but the five little children were most humane and would not use it. Not till the callous stable boy heaved a small rock at him did the pony burst into a vicious gallop. Nor was this enjoyable, for though the children found it exciting, the governess grew alarmed, her charges were flung from side to side, the cart pitched dangerously, and they nearly upset rounding the bend.

When the governess succeeded in controlling him, Sundae subsided sulkily into a slow walk. This stubborn beast absolutely refused to trot. Madly would he gallop or maddeningly would he dawdle, but he did not "choose to run." A bitter disappointment indeed to the five little children who had longed for a pony earnestly!

However, they had wanted a pony, they now had a pony; and even if he were not their ideal they must make the best of him. So every morning the pony and cart were brought to the door, the governess and the children climbed in and all started for a drive. But though everyone tried to make friends with Sundae, though they all coaxed and cajoled him as best they might, nobody could induce him to go at a pleasant pace. On jolly summer days when children all feel brisk and lively, it is a dull matter to go jogging along in a cloud of dust. The dogged pony would stump ahead and seemed to take no interest whatever in the excursion. Small wonder that the children became discontented and impatient at such disobliging behavior.

About a month after the advent of the pony, word came that a circus had arrived in a village some miles away, and one fine afternoon all set forth in the pony cart for a treat. It took them a long time to make the journey because Sundae walked very slowly the whole way. But they reached the grounds at last, and having hitched Sundae to a tree the group made their way inside the tent. When they had settled themselves in their seats, almost the first thing they noticed was a pony somewhat resembling Sundae, performing gracefully in the ring. The trainer whistled once and the pony stood on his hind legs. He whistled twice and the pony danced; three times, the pony lay down and rolled over. Then the trainer cracked his whip and, with a pretty toss of his head, the pony commenced to trot around the ring, stepping daintily and altogether behaving in a most exemplary manner. The five little children were enraptured.

"What a sweet-tempered pony!" cried the oldest child.

"What a lot of tricks he knows!" cried the next.

"How beautifully he trots!" cried the third.

"I wish Sundae would trot that way!" cried the fourth.

Then an idea struck the fifth!

"Maybe Sundae would trot if we cracked the whip!"

No sooner was the circus over than out they all rushed pell-mell and tumbled into the pony cart. Crack, went the whip in the air, and lo, with a toss of his mane, off trotted Sundae at an easy gliding pace. What was the delight of the children, as it dawned upon them that, instead of a sulky, mean-spirited steed, they had a thoroughly well-trained circus pony who had simply been waiting for his cue!

From that day on, Sundae was a constant source of amusement, as the children rapidly discovered his other accomplishments. Though the signals to which Sundae performed corresponded to those used by the trainer, the results were a bit different. Thus, at one whistle Sundae would waltz, at two whistles he would walk on his hind legs, while—astonishing to relate!—at the sight of a large red apple he would pirouette rapidly and sink to his knees. Moreover, it was accidentally found that he would sneeze three times for a lump of sugar. So, as you may easily imagine, the five little children lived happily ever after.

By Peggy Bacon

THE SEVEN WHITE CATS

THE seven white cats lived on a farm in Sandy Cove. It was a pleasant farm, halfway between the blue waters of the Bay of Fundy and the smiling waters of Saint Mary's Bay.

No one believed in the seven white cats until he had seen them. "Seven white cats? Ridiculous and absurd." That was what everyone said. But there were the cats, plainly to be seen if one took the trouble to walk up the hill to the farmhouse. Often Miranda, the farmer's little girl, would be sitting on the steps with all the cats around her.

It was Miranda who had given them their names. The mother of them all was Blue Eyes. The two half-grown kittens were the Angel Cat and the Odd Cat. The Angel Cat was a beautiful pure white with large blue eyes like her mother's; the Odd Cat was a trifle scrubby looking, and his eyes did not match, for one was blue and one was yellowish brown. Then there were the four smallest kittens, little balls of white fur, always tumbling over each other in the grass or chasing each other's tails. Three of them were Tim, Tip, and Tinker. The fourth was called Stub, because he had only a stub of a tail. The kittens had been brought up in the barn and, sad to relate, Stub's tail had been stepped on by one of the oxen!

Miranda was particularly fond of cats. Her father, Mr. Saunders, was not at all fond of cats, but he was fond of Miranda and so he allowed her to keep them. At least, he allowed her to keep them until one terrible day when everything went wrong. That day was indeed an unlucky one for the seven cats.

The trouble began almost before dawn, when Mr. Saunders went out to milk the cows. Stub, in spite of his accident, was always in the barn, and he ran right in front of Mr. Saunders, who tripped over him and dropped the milk pail. This made Mr. Saunders very angry.

Things kept on happening all through the day. When Mrs. Saunders went into the dairy, she found Blue Eyes helping herself to the biggest bowl of cream. Like other white cats with blue eyes, this cat was deaf, and she did not hear Mrs. Saunders coming. A little later in the day Tinker climbed up the lace curtains in the living room, and tore a large hole in one of them. Tip tangled himself up in Mrs. Saunders' knitting and Tim played havoc with her work basket.

"Cats are a nuisance!" said Mrs. Saunders.

"There are not going to be any cats on this farm," said Mr. Saunders.

"Oh, please, Papa!" said Miranda.

Mr. Saunders did not pay any attention to Miranda. When he made up his mind to be firm, he was very firm. That afternoon when Miranda was out visiting one of her friends, he bundled all seven white cats into a large crate, loaded the crate on the ox cart, along with baskets of vegetables, and started off. There was a great scuffling and miaowing. From one side of the crate came a white paw, and from the other two blue eyes looked out beseechingly. Mr. Saunders was very hard hearted.

First of all he drove up the hill to Miss Letty's house. Her adopted twins, Abigail and Sara, were delighted to have a white kitten. They chose Stub because they liked his funny short tail.

Then Mr. Saunders drove down the hill. There seemed to be only one place where he could leave the Angel Cat, that was at the parsonage. As luck would have it, there was the minister's wife, standing by the gray stone wall pruning her lilac bushes.

"This," said Mr. Saunders, "is the cat you need. Her name is Angel, most suitable for a parsonage cat. You will find her good company when the minister is writing his sermons."

Then Mr. Saunders drove on, leaving the minister's wife looking very much surprised, holding the **Angel Cat** in her arms.

Now Mr. Saunders was well on the road to Tiverton, a fishing village, where he intended to exchange his vegetables for dried fish. The oxen jogged slowly and steadily along. Mr. Saunders guided them with "Gee!" and "Haw!" and an occasional flick of his whip. He did not hurry them, for no one hurries in that part of the world.

Up the long hill they went, along the road until they came to the first village, which was Mink Cove. At one side of the road was a sturdy, neat house with a long patch of yellow tansy growing outside the gate. "I am quite sure these folks need a cat," said Mr. Saunders and, without stopping the oxen, he picked up Tinker and dropped him into the middle of the tansy patch. The oxen plodded on.

A little farther along the road there was a comfortable farmhouse with a large gray barn. A blue wooden cradle stood under the maple tree at the gate, and the farmer's little boy was helping his mother to tuck the baby into it.

"Such a nice family should have a cat," said Mr. Saunders. "Here is a white kitten, exactly the sort of kitten you would like." He held Tim up, so they could see him.

"We'd like to have a white kitten," said the rosy-cheeked farmer's wife. She came over and took Tim from Mr. Saunders. "Thank you very much. Don't you want him yourself?"

"No," said Mr. Saunders, "one white cat may be a very nice thing to own, but seven white cats—" and he drove on.

As the oxen plodded along the road, Mr. Saunders whistled cheerily, for now there were only three more cats. Soon he came to a cottage which looked different from all the other cottages, for instead of weathered shingles it had a bright red roof. The owner of the cottage had just finished painting it and he was standing with his paint pot and paint brush in his hand, admiring it.

"A house with a bright red roof always looks better if there is a white cat somewhere around," said Mr. Saunders. When the ox cart drove on again the man was holding his paint pot and paint brush in one hand and Tip in the other. He was astonished, for he had always thought he did not care for cats.

The oxen jogged on, and the sea came in sight. This was East Ferry, and in a cottage near the edge of the water lived an old lady who had a great deal of rheumatism. She was sitting by the window looking out at her garden and at the hollyhocks which were as tall as the house. Mr. Saunders jumped down from the cart, carried Blue Eyes over to the window, and dropped her into the old lady's lap, through the wide-open casement, while he stood outside.

"Here's fine company for you on winter evenings," said he. Then he drove on, leaving the old lady almost out of breath.

There was only one cat left, the Odd Cat, and Mr. Saunders was not at all sure that anyone would care to have a cat with such a strangely assorted pair of eyes. They were ferried across the water to Tiverton, where Mr. Saunders left his vegetables. There he found a fisherman who took the greatest fancy to the Odd Cat.

"Cats with eyes like those are lucky," said the fisherman.

Mr. Saunders sang happily as he turned the heads of his oxen toward home. He sang all the way from East Ferry to Tidville. He hummed all the way from Tidville to Little River. From Little River to Mink Cove he neither sang nor hummed, for he had begun to wonder what Miranda would say. From Mink Cove to Sandy Cove he felt very sad indeed.

When the ox cart stopped in front of his own farmhouse, Mr. Saunders saw Miranda sitting on the steps. Big tears were running down her cheeks and she gave her father a reproachful look. Mr. Saunders did not dare to say anything; he unyoked the oxen and took them into the barn.

Miranda's tears continued to flow. It seemed as if nothing in the world would stop them. While she ate her supper, big tears splashed into her bowl of bread and milk. While she fed the ducks and chickens, tears splashed into the dish of chicken feed. The tears were still trickling when Miranda went to bed, yet she said nothing at all.

"This is more than I can stand!" said Mr. Saunders.

"We must do something to make her forget those cats. We certainly must."

"I can't think what possessed you," remarked his wife, shaking her head mournfully.

"I don't know, myself," said Mr. Saunders.

The next morning Mr. Saunders told Miranda that he would take her to the lighthouse. Miranda had always wanted to go to the lighthouse, but she did not even smile. "Yes, Papa," was all she said, in a sad little voice.

It was a gray day. Fog blew in from the Bay of Fundy and almost hid the dark green fir trees. All the way to the lighthouse Miranda looked very sad. Mr. Saunders thought of the seven white cats and wished he had kept just one of them.

They drew near the lighthouse, on its rocky point, and Miranda began to be interested. The lighthouse was very white and neat, the rocks were very black and forbidding. The fog had rolled back over the Bay of Fundy, and sea and sky were blue once more. As they went up the path to the lighthouse a baby came toddling out of the door, a pink and gold baby who laughed and held out her hands to Miranda. Miranda smiled—just a little smile. The lighthouse keeper's wife came out to see that the baby was safe.

And then—a black and white cat came through the doorway. Behind her came four kittens: a black and white kitten, a black kitten, a gray kitten, and—last of all—a white kitten with blue eyes.

Miranda sat right down on the rocky ground and called the kitten. She picked it up and hugged it closely to her. For the first time that day she looked happy.

"Your little girl seems to be very fond of cats," said the lighthouse keeper's wife.

"She certainly is," answered Mr. Saunders, a trifle grimly.

Miranda sat and held the white kitten.

"Would you like to take my white kitty home with you?" asked the lighthouse keeper's wife.

"Yes! Oh, yes, I would!" answered Miranda. "May I, Papa?"

"I suppose so," sighed her father. "Now let's go and see the light."

Miranda would not let go of the white kitten even for a moment. She was much more interested in the kitten than she was in the funny little winding stairs inside the lighthouse, or in the great revolving light at the top. In fact she wanted to start for home as soon as possible.

As they came up the road to the farmhouse Miranda and Mr. Saunders could scarcely believe their eyes. There, sitting sedately on the doorstep, were Blue Eyes, the Odd Cat, and the Angel Cat. The four kittens scampered around in the grass.

"Why!" said Miranda. "Why, here are all the cats! They must have walked home." She gathered all the cats that she could hold into her arms and hugged them. "I'm so happy!" she said.

Mr. Saunders said nothing at all, but after that there were eight cats at the farmhouse. And all the way from Tiverton to Sandy Cove people said to each other, "Have you seen a white cat anywhere? We had one here the other day."

By Alice Dalgliesh

THE DOLL UNDER THE BRIAR ROSEBUSH

THERE was once a little girl, and her name was Beate. She was only five years old, but a bright and good little girl she was.

On her birthday her father had given her a beautiful straw hat. There were red ribbons around it, I can't tell you how pretty it was. Her mother had given her a pair of yellow shoes and the daintiest white dress. But her old aunt had given her the very best present of all; it was a doll, with a sweet pretty face and dark brown curls. She was a perfect beauty in every respect. There

was nothing the matter with her except that the left eyebrow was painted a tiny bit too high up.

"It looks as if she were frowning a little. I wonder if she is not quite pleased?" asked Beate, when she held her in her arms.

"Oh, yes," answered her aunt, "but she doesn't know you yet. It is a habit she has of always lifting her eyebrow a little when she looks closely at anyone. She only wants to find out if you are a good little girl."

"Yes, yes, and now she knows, for now that eyebrow is just like the other one," said Beate.

Oh, how Beate grew to love that doll, almost more than she loved Marie and Louise, and they were her best friends.

One day Beate was walking in the yard with her doll in her arms. The doll had a name now, and they had become fast friends. She had called her Beate, her own name, and the name of her old aunt who had given her the doll.

It was in the early spring. There was a beautiful green spot, with fine, soft grass in one corner of the yard around the old well. There stood a big willow tree with a low trunk, and it was covered with the little yellow blossoms that children call goslings.

They look like goslings too, for each little tassel has soft, soft yellow down, and they can swim in the water, but walk?—no, that they cannot do.

Now Big Beate—she wasn't more than five years old, but she was ever so much bigger than the other one— and Little Beate soon agreed that they would pick goslings from the tree and throw them into the well, so that they might have just as good a time as the big geese and goslings that were swimming about in the pond. It was really Big Beate who thought of this first, but Little Beate agreed immediately; you can't imagine how good she always was.

Now Big Beate climbed up into the willow and picked many pretty yellow goslings into her white apron, and when she counted them and had counted to twenty, twice, she said that now they had enough, and Little Beate thought so too.

So she began to climb down, but that was not easy for she had to hold her apron together with one hand and climb with the other. She thought Little Beate called up to her to throw the goslings down first, but she didn't dare to do that; she was afraid they might fall and hurt themselves.

Now both of them ran over to the well, and Big Beate helped her little friend to get her legs firmly fixed between the logs that were around the well, so that she might sit in comfort and watch the little goslings swim about on the water. Then gosling after gosling was dropped down, and as soon as each one reached the water it seemed to become alive and it moved about. Oh, what fun! Big Beate clapped her hands to the pretty little downy birds, and when she helped Little Beate a bit, she too could clap her hands.

But after awhile the little goslings would not swim any longer but lay quite still. That was no fun at all, so Big Beate asked her namesake if she didn't think she might lean a little over the edge of the well and blow on them, for then she thought they might come to life again. Little Beate didn't answer, but she raised her left eyebrow a good deal and moved her right arm in the air as if she were saying, "Please don't do that, dear Big Beate! Don't you remember Mother has told us how dark it is down there in the well? Think, if you should fall in!"

"Oh, nonsense; just see how easy it is," said Big Beate, for she thought the goslings were stupid when they didn't want to swim about. She leaned out over the well and blew on the nearest ones. Yes, it helped, the goslings began to swim again. But those that were farthest away didn't move at all.

"What stupid little things!" said Beate, and she leaned far, far out over the edge of the well. Then her little hands slipped on the smooth log and—splash! in she fell deep down into the water. It was so cold, so icy cold, and it closed over her head and took the straw hat, which she had got on her birthday, off her hair. She hadn't time to hear if Little Beate screamed, but I'm sure she did.

When Beate's head came over the water again she grasped the round log with both her hands but the hands were too small and the log too wide and slippery, she couldn't hold on. Then she saw her dear friend, Little Beate, standing stiff and dumb with fright, staring at her and with her right arm stretched out to her. Big Beate hurriedly caught hold of her and Little Beate made herself as stiff as she could, and stiffer still, and stood there between the logs holding her dear friend out of the water.

Now Beate screamed so loudly that her father and mother heard her and came running as fast as they could, pale and frightened, and pulled her out. She was dripping wet and so scared and cold that her teeth chattered.

The father ran to the house with her, but she begged him for heaven's sake not to leave Little Beate, for she might fall into the well, "And it's she who has saved me."

Now they put Beate to bed and Little Beate had to sleep with her. When she had said her prayers she hugged her little friend and said, "Never, never can I thank you enough, because you saved me from that horrible deep well, dear Little Beate. Of course, I know that our Lord helped you to stand firm between the logs, and to make yourself so strong and stiff, but it was you, and no one else who stretched your hand out to me, so that I was not drowned. And therefore you shall be my very best friend, always, and when I grow up you shall be the godmother to my first daughter, and I shall call her Little Beate for you." Then she kissed the little one and slept.

By Gudrun Thorne-Thomsen

THE DINNER BELL

ONCE upon a time there was a large rambling farm-house. It was a beautiful old house, with a lovely front door and beams of strong oak, with a big fireplace in the parlor and a big fireplace in the sitting room.

The children, Edward and Jane, thought it was the nicest house in the whole world. The big dog, Jerry, thought it was the nicest house in the whole world.

One of the interesting things about it was the dinner bell. It was a big bell that hung in a framework of wood on the very top of the kitchen roof. Every day at noon time the bell was rung to tell the men in the fields that dinner was ready. Every day at supper time it was rung to tell them that supper was ready. The dinner bell was rung by pulling a rope that was fastened to it and hung down by the side of the house outside the kitchen door.

One day Mother said, "It is nearly noon. You may ring the dinner bell, Edward."

Edward reached up and took the rope from the hook on which it hung. He pulled it back and forth and the bell on the roof went: "Ding, dong! Ding, dong! Ding, dong!"

Loud and clear it rang over the fields and meadows. Jerry stood with upturned face watching every move as Edward pulled the rope.

Over and over Edward pulled the rope. Over and over the beautiful tones rang out through the sunshiny air. When Edward noticed the eager look on the dog's face, he asked, "Would you like to ring the bell, Jerry?" He placed the rope between Jerry's teeth and the dog pulled on it. To his delight the bell rang. "You can ring the bell as well as anybody, can't you?" said Edward.

Jerry held his head proudly and wagged his tail happily as he kept ringing the bell. When it had been rung enough, Edward put the rope back on the hook. At once Jerry stood on his hind feet and tried to reach it.

"No, Jerry, you mustn't ring the bell any more," declared Edward. "You must never ring it unless I give you permission."

Down in the cornfield Father heard the dinner bell. "That is a pleasant sound," he thought. "I am as hungry as a dog." He unhitched the horse from the cultivator, drove him up the lane, put him in the barn and gave him his dinner of oats and hay. Then he went toward the house.

Edward's big brother, Charles, heard the bell. "That is a pleasant sound," he thought. "I am as hungry as a bear." He hung his hoe on the fence and started to the house.

Andrew, the hired man, who was mending a fence near the far end of the farm, heard the bell. "That is a pleasant sound," he thought. "I am as hungry as a wolf." He laid his tools down in a fence corner and started for the house.

Jane, who was playing in the front yard, heard the dinner bell. She took a doll under each arm and went into the house for dinner.

Jerry welcomed each one with a friendly look and a happy wag of his tail as they came onto the porch.

But Father did not come into the house at once. He stood looking up at the roof. He saw something that he had never noticed before. When he did come to the dinner table, he remarked, "The framework that the bell hangs in is rotting away. One of the pieces has fallen apart. I will get some new lumber soon and we will repair it. Some day the bell might come tumbling down."

"Why mend it?" Mother inquired. "You men all have watches now. It is a bother to remember to ring the bell on time. When Edward isn't here I have to leave my cooking and ring it myself."

"Let us take the old bell down," remarked Charles. "What is the use of it any more?"

"I like to hear it ring," said little Jane.

"I agree with you, Jane," Father said. "I like to hear the dinner bell ring. Ever since I was a boy I have heard it. But if it is a bother to have it rung and we don't really need it any more, we might as well take it down. We'll do it next week, when the haying is finished."

Now Edward spoke. "I like to ring it and Jerry likes to ring it. He rang it today."

"Of all things!" exclaimed Charles. "So Jerry can ring the dinner bell, can he?"

"Perhaps we had better keep it after all," admitted Mother, when she saw how much Father and the children liked it. "It might come in handy sometime."

"All right," agreed Father. "We'll mend the framework and leave the bell up there."

— 116 —

The next three days Edward and Jerry rang the bell. Indeed, once Jerry rang it alone. And a happier dog there never was, as one could tell by the quickness with which he ran to do it when Edward called.

After dinner on the third day, Mother said, "I wish you would stay and look after the house for an hour or two, Edward, while I go to call on Mrs. Brown, who is sick."

"All right," Edward replied. "Jerry and I will stay."

The men went to their work in the fields. They were making hay that day. Mother took Jane with her to the neighbor's. Everything was quiet around the place. Only the buzzing of flies on the back porch, the humming of bees in the honeysuckle, and the twittering of birds in the trees could be heard.

Edward lay down on the grass under a tree, for he was tired after following the mower around all the forenoon. Before one could wink ten times he was asleep. Half an hour later he was awakened by the barking of a dog. In a moment Jerry came running to him, barking as he ran.

"Why are you barking, Jerry?" he asked.

In another moment Edward knew, for out of the door and out of the windows of the kitchen smoke came pouring.

"Oh! The house is on fire!" he shouted. But no one heard.

Edward ran to the door and looked in. Back of the stove little flames were bursting out of the wall. He grabbed a pail half full of water and tried to throw it on the fire. It did not reach quite high enough; the fire kept on burning.

There was another pail of water on the kitchen table. Edward tried to lift that, but he was only eight and the big pail of water was too heavy for him. He threw a dipper full of water on the fire, but such a tiny bit of water could not put it out.

"I can never put the fire out alone," he thought. He shouted, "Fire! Fire!" But no one heard him, for no one was near. Then he called to Jerry, "Ring the dinner bell, Jerry. Ring the dinner bell."

Down in the hayfield all at once the men heard a bell above the sound of the hay rake. Father, who was pitching hay into little haycocks, stopped with his pitchfork poised in the air.

"Why—that sounds like our dinner bell!" he exclaimed.

"Sure enough," said Charles. "I wonder what the trouble is."

Andrew stopped the horse and listened. "Oh, there is no trouble," he protested. "Maybe Jerry is ringing it for fun."

"He might be," Charles agreed. "It would be a good thing to have the old bell taken down. Then he couldn't ring it in the middle of the afternoon and scare us all."

"But there might be some trouble," said Father. "Edward wouldn't let Jerry ring it for nothing. Come, let's all go to the house."

"All right," said Charles, and he started off.

"Hitch the horse to the fence and follow us," Father called to Andrew.

When they were almost at the head of the lane they saw smoke pouring out of the house. Soon they were throwing water on the fire.

Mother heard the dinner bell as she was talking with the neighbor.

"Dear me! That is our dinner bell!" she exclaimed. "What can the matter be?"

She started home. Neighbors heard the bell and ran to find out the trouble. They all helped put out the fire. Some of the men pumped water from the well. Some carried pails of water and threw it on the fire. The flames died down. The fire went out.

All the time the bell kept ringing. When they were through fighting the fire, there was Jerry still happily pulling the rope.

"Just see how they all come when I ring the bell," he was thinking.

"It is a good thing Edward was here to start throwing water on the fire," said Father. "It might have become so big that we could not have stopped it. He saved our nice old house."

"I couldn't have done it alone," said Edward. "If Jerry had not helped by ringing the bell to call the rest of you, the house would have burned."

"Good dog," said Charles, as he patted Jerry's neck.

"If the bell had not been here, Jerry could not have rung it and none of us would have known there was a fire," said Mother.

"Maybe we had better not take it down," remarked Charles.

"You are right," Father agreed. "We'll make a strong, new frame and let the old dinner bell keep hanging there."

"And we'll let Edward and Jerry be the bell ringers," said Mother.

By Helen Fuller Orton

THE BARN

ONCE there was a barn. It was a big red barn and it stood on a hill for all who passed to see. It was much bigger than the little white farmhouse by its side. But it was not nearly so tall as the old elm tree on its other side. Between the little white house and the tall green tree, the barn on the hill showed big and red.

It was a barn full of pleasant smells. At night the sixteen black and white Holstein cows stood in the stalls with their heads through the stanchions. Then the barn smelled of their warm breath. And if it was cold so that they stayed in the barn all night long, the barn seemed warm and friendly to the farmer when he came in the early frosty morning. When the farmer had milked these sixteen cows, strained the foamy white milk, separated it in the separator and poured it into great cans, then the barn smelled of the warm fresh milk.

The six little calves in their pen at the end of the barn smelled this sweet smell of fresh milk and mooed and capered with excitement. For they knew that soon the farmer's boy would bring them their breakfast—a big pail full of skimmed milk for each! Into each pail goes a little pink nose while all the pairs of funny, wobbly, black and white legs spread wide to brace the eager little creatures. Gulp, gulp, gulp, down goes the milk! The little bull calf with the two black ears is through first. Stand back! He is going to throw his pail! He raises it on the end of his nose hoping to get another drop. The pail is dry. So bang, away it goes! But he is still hungry.

He smells that delicious smell in the next pail. He bunts the little calf next to him, trying to get his own nose into the pail. But that calf is just as hungry as he is. What a squabble! Bang! bang! two more pails are empty. Bang, bang, bang! the six pails have all been tossed away and six long pink tongues are hard at work licking lips, noses, ears—anything that has a trace of the good white milk. No smell so good as the smell of fresh milk to a hungry calf. And twice every day after milking, the big red barn is filled with this sweet smell.

The little pointed-winged swallow whose nest was just above Buttercup's stall did not like milking time so well as the calves did. She swooped—a steel-blue flash—in and out, chattering and twittering with anxiety. When the cows were out in the meadow grazing, she had the place to herself. For she did not count the farmer or the farmer's boy. They cleaned out the stalls and fussed around the separator without disturbing her at all. Hundreds of times each day when she had been building her nest, she had flitted with a long swoop through the open door to the beam on the low ceiling, bringing a tiny speck of mud or a straw. That was weeks ago.

Now, the little mud home was dry and lined with her soft feathers. And in it lay five speckled eggs! No wonder she was nervous when those sixteen big black and white cows came lumbering into the barn! But she never moved. She sat with her pointed tail and forked wings covering the precious eggs. No, she would not move, not even when Buttercup stretched out her neck and gave a big Moo-oo-oo-oooooo! right under her. Perhaps she knew that Buttercup was only telling the farmer that her bag was very full and please to hurry and milk her. Just the quivering chestnut throat of the little bird and the beadlike eyes showed above the mud rim of the nest.

And down at the other end of the barn, the two big work horses were waiting for the smell that meant supper to them. Hay! Sweet-smelling hay! Up in the loft the air was thick with its fragrance. Great piles rose nearly to the cobwebbed rafters—soft, springy piles that gave as you walked, let you sink way down but sort of threw you back again. Stray wisps of hay hung here and there, for once the piles had been higher still. Much had been thrown down the hole in the floor to the room below, where the cows and horses lived. The pitchfork with its long, sharp prongs always stood ready for the farmer or his boy. It could hold a big bunch of hay on those long prongs!

Haying time—that was when the pitchfork was busiest. Out in the fields the grass lay in heaps slowly turning into hay in the sun. "Yesterday's flowers" and grass —that is what hay is—yesterday's flowers and grass dried in the sun, pitched up onto a hay wagon by the farmers and often by their wives and children, driven by the work horses to the barn with the haymakers sitting high on top of the rounded heap on the wagon, then pitched from the wagon to the hayloft and left to be the winter dinners for the horses and cows. Grass and flowers and sun—no wonder hay smells fragrant and sweet!

There are other and smaller animals that go sniffing around this barn of pleasant smells. They have little whiskered noses and long tails and they love to make nests in the sweet-smelling hay for their squirming pink babies. They are really little field mice, and when it is warm summer time they make their nests and raise their pink squirming babies in the long grass of the fields. But when the weather is nipping, they like to move into the spacious, warm hayloft and make little nest houses for themselves in yesterday's flowers and grass. I wonder which house—of the green or of the sun-dried grass —the little squirming babies like better?

And the little mice have big cousins in the barn, with longer whiskered noses and longer tails and bigger pink squirming babies. Mice noses and rat noses will sniff out the corn, and mice teeth and rat teeth will nibble the feed that the farmer has meant for the chickens—or they will if he doesn't take care!

But in this big red barn on the hill, the farmer has taken care. At night when our eyes can see only dimly if at all, the mice eyes and the rat eyes can see quite plainly the little hole just where the wall joins the floor into the grain room. Sharp mice teeth and sharp rat teeth have gnawed this little hole because whiskered mice noses and whiskered rat noses smelled the corn inside. And every night there is a patter of little rat feet and littler mice feet through the hole into the grain room. Always they hope. Yet always, when they follow the tempting smell of the corn, they come to a place where there are smooth, round posts. But mice feet and rat feet have sharp claws, and up the posts the little creatures swarm, their whiskers wiggling with delight.

But—what is this they find? A great overhanging disc, like an umbrella! Try as they will, they cannot get over it, they cannot reach that wonderful smell. It is just beyond that disc. It might as well be at the North Pole! The farmer knew what he was doing when he put those overturned tin pans on the posts of the table that held his corn. The hens and the roosters and the chickens that belong to that big red barn need not worry. Their delicious-smelling corn is safe from the eager little mice and rats!

Are the little mice and their rat cousins safe themselves? There are other soft-padded feet in the big red barn. There are other bright eyes that see in the dark. There is another and bigger whiskered nose that smells a smell that means "dinner." That is the smell of the mice and the rats themselves! For old Tom, the cat—he too prowls around the big red barn at night. And a smart old cat he is, as many a frightened squeak at night tells. Look out, little mice, that when you are hunting for dinner, you are not hunted for dinner yourselves, that when you are sniffing the delicious smell of corn, you are not yourself being sniffed by old Tom!

So the animals live in the big red barn that stands on a hill for all who pass to see. The sixteen black and white Holstein cows, the six hungry little black and white calves, the steel-blue barn swallow, the two big work horses, the many little field mice and their bigger rat cousins, and old Tom the cat. Between the little white house where the farmer, the farmer's wife and farmer's boy live and the overarching elm tree where the orioles have built a swinging house and the chattering gray squirrels leap, there stands the big red barn. A good home for all the animals it houses, is this barn of pleasant smells!

By Lucy Sprague Mitchell

WILLIAM AND JANE

WILLIAM liked it standing still. When he was hoeing or raking or planting seeds or picking peas he stood just as still as he could. Even when he ran he looked as though almost any minute he'd be standing still again. That's the way William was.

Jane wasn't that way, though. She liked it hopping and skipping and jumping and climbing and crawling under and wriggling over and squirming through.

"William," Jane would say to him, "why do you like it so much standing still?"

"Well," William would say very slowly, "well, Jane, because I do. Why do you like it so much hopping and skipping about?"

"Oh, because I do," Jane would say, and go running off somewhere else to play.

One day Jane had an idea. "William," she said, "how would it be if for one whole day you went skipping and hopping about the way I do and I went around standing almost still the way you do? How would that be?"

"Well," said William, "why?"

"For fun," said Jane. "To surprise my mother and

father," said Jane, "and the twins and the twins' nurse and cook."

"Well," said William, "all right." And he went on very slowly pulling up some beets. After he had finished pulling them he put them in his basket and very, very slowly stood up straight again.

"Well," he said, "when had we better start?"

"Tomorrow morning." Jane gave a little skip. "I'll begin the first thing I get up and you begin the first thing you get up."

"Well, all right," said William, "but I don't think I'll like it very much." And he went off toward the kitchen with his beets.

The next morning when Jane got up she didn't jump out of her bed the way she usually did. No. Instead she shoved one foot out very slowly from underneath the covers, and sat and looked at it.

"Jane," said her mother, who had come in to help her button her back waist buttons, "why aren't you getting up?"

"Well," said Jane slowly, the way William said things, "I . . . am. . . ." And she poked her other foot very slowly from underneath the covers and sat and looked at *it*.

"What's the matter with Jane?" called Jane's father from the next room, where he was neatly lacing up his shoes. "I don't hear her getting up."

"I don't know," called back Jane's mother. "She's acting very queerly. I wish you'd come and see."

So Jane's father came and looked at Jane too. They both stood and looked at Jane looking at her feet.

"Get up, Jane," said her father.

"Get *up,* Jane," said her mother.

"I'm counting, Jane," said her father. "One, two, three, four, five . . ."

But suddenly Jane's father saw something out the window.

"Goodness," he said, instead of saying six.

What he saw was William washing off the furniture in the garden. But William wasn't doing it slowly and carefully, standing still in between washes the way he generally did. No. Instead he was hopping and skipping about waving his sponge and his pail.

"William," called Jane's father from the window, "whatever is the matter?"

"Oh, nothing," called back William. "I'm just hopping. Tra-la, tra-la-la-la."

"This is very queer," said Jane's father. And he and Jane's mother ran downstairs and out into the garden. They ran as fast as they could, but when they got there William had stopped washing furniture and was off skipping underneath the cherry trees.

"William," called Jane's mother, "whatever are you doing?"

"Oh, just skipping," cried William. "Tra-la, tra-la-la-la."

"Well!" said Jane's father and mother.

And they both went in to breakfast so surprised.

"Where's Jane?" asked cook when she brought in the cereal.

"She isn't dressed yet, cook," said Jane's mother. "I don't know what's the matter with her. When we came down she was just sitting and looking at her feet. Do you suppose she's still sitting and looking at her feet?"

"I hope not," said Jane's father, "but I'd better go and see."

"Jane," he called from the foot of the stairs, "are you still sitting and looking at your feet or are you putting shoes on them?"

"No . . . Father," said Jane very slowly, from a long way off. "No . . . Father . . . I'm . . . still . . . looking . . . at . . . them . . . but . . . I . . . have . . . a . . . stocking . . . in . . . my . . . hand . . . and . . . pretty soon . . . I'm . . . going . . . to . . . put . . . it . . . on."

"I can't imagine what's the matter with Jane," said Jane's father, coming back to his cereal. "She's never been this way before. I wonder if we shouldn't call the doctor."

"The doctor?" asked Jane's mother.

But just then William went by the window. He was going down toward the garden with his hose to water

the flowers. But he wasn't going down to the garden with his hose the way he generally went down to the garden with his hose. No. Instead he was playing skip rope with it.

"William!" cried Jane's father, rushing to the door. And *"William!"* cried Jane's mother and cook, rushing to the door.

But William didn't even look at them. He went right on playing skip rope with his hose.

"Why, this is dreadful," said Jane's father, going back to his breakfast once more, "William acting the way he is and Jane acting the way *she* is. I don't know what to think of it, do you?"

"No," said Jane's mother, "I can't think *what* to think."

"Well," said Jane's father finally, "I'll tell you what. After I've gone to work you'd better telephone me at my office and tell me just what's happening."

"All right," said Jane's mother, "I will."

So then Jane's father went upstairs to kiss Jane good-by.

Jane was standing still in the middle of the room when he came in. She had one stocking on and was looking at her shoes.

"Why, Jane"—Jane's father stared at her—"we've finished breakfast and I'm all ready to go to my office, and here you still are."

"Well . . . yes . . . here . . . I . . . still . . . am . . ." said Jane.

"Why, Jane," said her father again.

Then he couldn't wait any longer to talk to her, because he was late. So he kissed her good-by.

"Don't forget to telephone," he called to Jane's mother, and ran down the street.

After he'd been at his office about an hour the telephone rang. It was Jane's mother.

"Jane has both stockings on now," she said, "and she's started with her shirt."

"She's only as far as her *shirt?*" asked Jane's father.

"Yes," said Jane's mother, "and William's raked a pile of leaves and now he's rolling in them."

"*Rolling* in them?" asked Jane's father.

"Yes," said Jane's mother, "around and around."

"Oh," said Jane's father, "how awful!"

"Yes," said Jane's mother. "Good-by."

So then Jane's father went back to his work. He talked to some men, and wrote his name on papers, and opened letters with his knife. But all the time he was thinking about William and Jane.

About lunch time the telephone rang again.

"Jane has her shirt on," said Jane's mother, "and she's lacing up one shoe."

"Just her shirt and her shoe since you called me last time?" asked Jane's father.

Jane's mother sounded sad: "Just her shirt and her shoe."

"And what's William doing?" asked Jane's father.

"William's crawling under the porch," said Jane's mother.

"Why?" asked Jane's father.

"I don't know," said Jane's mother. "All I can see is his feet."

"Oh," said Jane's father, "how awful!"

"Yes," said Jane's mother. "Good-by."

So then Jane's father went back to his work again. He signed his name some more, and blotted it, and threw lots and lots of papers on the floor. But all the time he was thinking about William and Jane. All afternoon he thought: "How dreadful it is to have William acting the way he is and Jane acting the way she is. I do wish Jane's mother would call me again . . ."

Pretty soon she did.

"Hello," said Jane's father when the telephone rang, "hello, hello."

"Hello," said Jane's mother. Her voice was quite weak.

"What's happening?" asked Jane's father.

"Jane has on her waist," said Jane's mother, "and her panties and one shoe, and now she's putting on her dress."

"Do you think she'll be dressed before it's time for her to go to bed?" asked Jane's father.

"I don't know," said Jane's mother.

"But what shall we do if she isn't dressed by the time it's time for her to get *undressed* again?"

"Oh, I don't know," said Jane's mother. "But won't you please hurry home?"

"What's William doing?" asked Jane's father.

"He's up in a tree," said Jane's mother. "Won't you please hurry home?"

"I'll come right away," said Jane's father. "Goodby."

So he hurried home as fast as he could, and when he got inside the gate he looked up in all the tops of the trees for William.

— 131 —

"William," he called. "William! Come down, William. Nice William. Come down."

But William wasn't in a tree. No, William was leaning against the side of the house with his head hanging over.

"Why, William," said Jane's father, "Jane's mother just telephoned me that you were up in a tree, so I hurried home to get you down again. Why did you climb up a tree, William?"

"Well," said William very slowly, "I wish I never had."

"Are you sorry that you did it, William?" asked Jane's father.

"Yes," said William, "very."

"And you won't climb up trees or roll in hay or hop or skip or jump rope any more the way you did today?"

"No," said William, "never. What I feel like doing," he said, "is standing very still for a long, long time." And he began to do it.

Then Jane's father went to look for Jane. He found her in her mother's room. She was all dressed with her hair ribbon on and both shoes laced. And she was skipping as hard as she could.

"Hello, Father," she said without stopping her skipping.

"Hello, Jane," said her father.

"I'm all dressed now," said Jane, giving her father a kiss without stopping her skipping.

"Isn't it funny? Suddenly she got dressed very quickly," said Jane's mother, "and started this skipping."

"I'm hopping now," said Jane. And she was.

"And pretty soon I'm going to jump," she said. And

she did. And then she started climbing up, and crawling under and wriggling over, and squirming through. Just the way she always used to do.

"I'm never going to stand still again," said Jane.

And she never, never did.

By Dorothy Aldis

BIG TREE

SUMMER

ONE bright sunny morning in summer Sally looked out
of the window of her room and cried, "Oh, Mother,
come and see the big tree! It is waving at me!"

Mother came to the window and looking out into the
lovely green branches that were blowing in the wind
said, "That is a big tree, isn't it? And it really looks as
though it were waving at you."

Sally had just moved into a new home with her
mother, her father, and her brother, Billy. The new
home was a cozy-looking little white house with green
shutters, green doors, and a green roof. Across the front
on one side of the house was a white picket fence. There
was a little gate that went "clickety-click" when it was
opened and "c-lock" when it was swung shut.

There were many trees in the yard. There was a little
aspen tree that always looked sparkly in the sunshine because its glossy round leaves fluttered continually from
morning till night. There were large maple trees and
tall oak trees. Then not far from the house there were
fruit trees—one with bright red cherries and one with
big apples. Near the fence was a little blue spruce tree,
and next to the blue spruce was Big Tree.

After breakfast, while Sally's mother was arranging
furniture in her new home, Sally and Billy played in
the yard. In the afternoon they carried Sally's doll
house to a shady place and that shady place was under
Big Tree. Sally and Billy played that the dolls were
going to move. They were just beginning to take out

the doll furniture when they heard "clickety-click" ana the "c-lock"! Father had come home.

Sally and Billy left the doll house and went with Father for a walk through the yard. First they went to the aspen tree and, as they came up to it, a little wren flew out of a wren house that was perched on a bough of the tree.

"A wren, a wren," called Billy.

"A squirrel, a squirrel," called Sally at the same time, for she saw a squirrel run to the oak tree. The squirrel ran a little way up the oak tree then stopped to look at Billy and Sally. It ran a little higher up then stopped to look at Father. Then it ran briskly up to the tiptop of the tree. Just as it disappeared in the leaves of the tree there was a "plippity-plop-plop" and down through the leaves came some brown acorns.

"Now I know why squirrels like this tree," said Sally.

Father said, "The oak tree grows something the squirrel likes to eat. Can you see a tree that has on it something we like to eat?"

"The cherry tree," said Billy.

"The apple tree," said Sally.

"You are both right," said Father.

"May we get some and eat them?" said Sally and Billy.

"The cherries are ripe but the apples are not," Father said. He held Sally up high so that she could pick some cherries. And he held Billy up so that he could pick some cherries.

Then Sally said, "Let's eat our cherries up in Big Tree." Sally and Billy showed Father the low branch of Big Tree to which they could easily climb, where

— 135 —

there was a fine place to sit. In a minute they were happily sitting in Big Tree eating their cherries.

The next minute Father said, "Run, children, it is

going to rain." Father, Billy, and Sally ran into the house. The rain poured down.

"My doll house, my furniture, my dolls! They will get all wet," said Sally.

As soon as the rain stopped Sally ran out to get her dolls. Imagine her surprise when she found them scarcely wet at all. Big Tree protected them.

That night when Sally was in bed she thought about the rain and Big Tree. Outside the wind was blowing and she heard Big Tree's branches gently strike the window pane as if it were trying to get in to say something to her. It was like having a friend near by to hear the tapping on her window pane.

AUTUMN

Before long the days grew colder and shorter. It was autumn. Big Tree was beautiful to see. The green leaves had turned to gay red, orange, yellow, and brown. But Sally was troubled. The gay-colored leaves were dropping from the tree.

"Is Big Tree dying?" said Sally one day to her mother.

"Oh, no," said Mother, "Big Tree is not dying, but soon it will lose its leaves and will have bare branches all winter. In the spring, however, new leaves will come. Wait until spring then you will see. The leaves work hard all summer making food for the tree. They have stopped working now, but much food is stored in the tree for the winter. The work of the leaves is over for a while. That is why they turn beautiful colors and drop from the tree."

Just then Billy called, "Hurry down, Sally, we are going to get apples today." After breakfast Sally and Billy helped Father gather apples.

"Now each choose the apple you would like to eat," said Father. It did not take long for the children to find the apples they wanted, but it did take them a long time to eat the apples. Sally and Billy loved to sit in the Big Tree.

One moonlight night, as Sally lay in bed, she saw something moving on the wall of her room. It was Big Tree. Big Tree was not in the room, but Big Tree's shadow was. Sally liked to watch it and, until she went to sleep, her eyes followed the swaying branches dancing on the wall.

WINTER

Winter came. The days were very short and very cold. Sally and Billy played outdoors after school nearly every day, but on stormy days they stayed inside. Sometimes they sat in front of the open fire and ate nuts and apples that had been gathered from their own trees.

One morning, when Sally looked out of her window, she could not see the black bare branches of Big Tree. They were covered with ice and sparkled in the sun like glass. Big Tree was a beautiful sight to see.

"Big Tree looks all crickly crackly," said Sally. "I wish it would stay that way." It did stay that way all day for it was very cold.

One evening before Christmas Father called Sally and Billy to the window as they were starting for bed. "Now close your eyes," said Father, "and don't look until I say 'ready.' " Father put up the window shade and said "ready." The children opened their eyes and looked right out into the little blue spruce. It was covered with colored lights—red ones, orange ones, yellow ones, and green ones.

"That is the prettiest Christmas tree we have ever seen," said Sally and Billy, as they went up to bed.

SPRING

"Today we can tap the maple tree," said Father one early spring morning to Sally and Billy. The children had great fun helping Father hang the buckets on the spouts which Father had put on the trees. Before long they heard "drip, drip, drip" in the bucket. It took a long time for the pail to fill up, but when it was filled the children carried it into the house and Father showed them how to make maple sugar of it. Sally and Billy thought it was wonderful.

Later in the spring something happened that Sally thought more wonderful than that. Tender green leaves were bursting from buds on all branches of Big Tree.

"Oh, Mother," said she, "come see Big Tree's new leaves." Mother came and as she and Sally were looking at the tree a robin flew to one of its branches.

Then Sally said, "I like our aspen tree; the wrens live in it. I like the oak tree; the squirrel lives in it. I like the fruit trees; they give us cherries and apples. I like the nut tree because it gives us nuts, and I like the maple tree because it gives us maple sugar. The little blue spruce is pretty and green all winter; I like it, but I *love* Big Tree! Mother, see! Big Tree is waving at me!"

By Marjorie Hardy

OCEAN AND SHORE

ON THE shores the waves are breaking. There they batter against rough rocks. The spray leaps white and falls in a mist. The rocks shine with slipperiness and the seaweed swishes.

On the shores the waves are breaking. There they roll out smooth on the hard-pounded sand—smooth and glassy with an edging of white foam—one, then another, and another—always another, down the dazzling stretch of the long beach.

On the shores the waves are breaking. There they throw themselves against the firm wall of the breakwater. In from the ocean, they crash and rush at the outer wall. The high-tossed water falls. Some of it slipping over the top flows in smooth little cataracts over into the calm waters of the harbor.

On the shores the waves are breaking. Here they are gentle. They come lap, lapping against the piers of the dock, lap, lapping against the sides of the anchored fishing boats, lap, lapping against the great iron wall of the ocean liner. The waves that break on the harbor shores are gentle waves. For men need safe and gentle waters for their harbor work. And the shores of the harbors are busy with the work of many men.

On the shores the waves are breaking—forever breaking. On the shores the men are working—forever working. Where the land leaves off and the sea begins, there is ever the sound of moving waters and the sound of working men.

By Lucy Sprague Mitchell

ONE evening while Mr. Mistletoe was pulling up plantain weeds . . .

But before we go on I had better tell you a few details about Mr. Mistletoe's adventures as a grass grower.

He was always happy when he was mowing the lawn —though lawn is certainly too smooth a word for such a bumpy arrangement of ground. There is something very soothing in the whir of the twirling blades, if it is not broken too often by the hard shock of a stick or a pebble or one of Donny's old bones. Keeping the lawn-mower straight, and enjoying the smell of cut grass, and feeling your own strong earth solid under your feet, is a healthy pleasure.

But though Mr. Mistletoe was very happy mowing the grass, he looked serious. Perhaps he was thinking? Certainly there was plenty to think about. I wonder what there was about his ground that made it so attractive to moles. Every time he thought he had got the front grass plot in pretty good order, there appeared a new lot of their wrinkly little subways. Then these soft tunnels had to be all carefully trodden down or else flattened out with the heavy roller. Worst of all was when Donny and Fritz would decide to give some help in the mole problem. Then, when Mr. Mistletoe came back in the evening, he would find a ragged zigzag furrow, ten or fifteen feet long, dug up one of the terraces. These excavations were worse to repair than all the tunnels a whole family of moles could make in a month.

Another thing Mr. Mistletoe used to think about, as he went solemnly to and fro with the lawnmower (stopping now and then to light his pipe and wipe his forehead) was the idea of starting a Nassau County Weed Show. In a flower show he would have no chance at all; but in a well-conducted weed show he ought to get a prize. His plantain weeds were remarkable, both in number and size. And in a good weed show there should also be prizes for the greatest number of croquet hoops lost in one season, or balls disappeared among rhododendron bushes, or velocipedes left out over night. In such competitions, he believed, the family would rank high.

But the plantain weeds were his special concern. On warm evenings he often spent an hour or so grubbing them up. Sometimes it seemed as though the lawn was really more plantain than grass. But it is quite good fun pulling them up, because you are never sure whether the roots will come or not. If you are careful to get hold of all the leaves, and give a little twist, the chances are that the roots will come too. The game is to keep score, and count how many roots come and how many don't.

What bothered Mr. Mistletoe, in these adventures, was that anything so plentiful as those weeds should be so useless. For he liked to imagine that almost everything is useful in one way or another if you understand about it. It always gave him great pain to throw anything away: he carefully preserved bits of string, heads of broken dolls, small pencils, buttons, corks, rusty nails. He rarely put these odds and ends to any purpose, but it made him happy to have saved them.

One evening, then, as I started to say at the beginning, Mr. Mistletoe was cheerfully pulling up plantain weeds and putting them into a basket. When the basket was full he carried it into the woods and dumped it, and doing so he had to pass by the rabbit run. As he did so, he always said "Well, bunny bunny bunny," which was not an important thing to say but showed a friendly spirit. He and the rabbits led very different lives, and perhaps they did not really have very much in common, but at any rate they were on good terms. So he was shocked, passing their wire netting, to see that their eyes were full of tears.

They were white rabbits, with beautiful red eyes. Even in their cheerfullest moods there seems something a little wistful about eyes of that color: they look as though they had been reddened by long and inconsolable weeping. So when you take eyes that are naturally red, and fill them with real tears, the effect is very sad. Mr. Mistletoe was painfully startled and stopped by the netting to wonder.

If he had not been rather a stupid man he would have guessed long before. The rabbits had been trying all summer to tell him, but he could not understand their language. It was gradually breaking their hearts to see him, day after day, pulling up and throwing away the beautiful delicious plantain weeds they love so much. Among the many things that Mr. Mistletoe did not know was the interesting fact that juicy green plantain is one of a rabbit's most favorite foods. And to remain helpless in their inclosure and watch all that plantain being wasted was more than they could bear.

When he stood there, holding the basket of weeds and wondering, the rabbits became greatly excited. Their ruby eyes glistened with trouble, their tall pink ears quivered, they stood up poking through the wire with noses that twitched.

"Good gracious," said Mr. Mistletoe. "They seem terribly upset about something. Can it be that they want some of the plantain? It might be very bad for them."

It seems queer that a man could be so ignorant. Do dogs like bones? Do horses like apples? Do Chinamen like rice? Do girls like fudge? That is how rabbits feel about plantain.

The behavior of the rabbits was so emphatic, their eyes were so eloquently wet, that Mr. Mistletoe thought

he might give them just one plantain and see what happened. When he began pushing it through the hole in the netting they almost tore it from his hands. There was a violent nibbling and crunching and in half a minute that green weed had entirely disappeared, even the little cluster of roots.

Mr. Mistletoe watched anxiously. He had a sort of

idea that perhaps Binny and Bunny would suddenly fall dead. But they looked stronger and bigger than ever, their noses trembled with healthy vibrations, the tears had vanished from their eyes. They looked at him in a way he could not possibly misunderstand.

Good heavens, he said to himself, and gave them the whole basket.

Late that night Mr. Mistletoe was waked by a queer soft cheerful sound coming from the back yard. The rabbits were singing.

Slowly and quietly Mr. Mistletoe thought about this matter. He noticed, after that, that every time he began to pull up plantain weeds the rabbits were watching him closely. Then a great idea came to him. He hunted about in the attic until he found the old baby pen that had been used by the children long ago. He carried it outdoors and put it over the richest and thickest patch of plantain on the lawn. Then he put Binny and Bunny in the pen. There was a merry sound of crisp eating, and that was the end of that patch. As they ate, the rabbits' active paws patted down the earth smoothly and neatly so that all was left tidy. After an hour's time he shifted the pen to another place and they began afresh.

So that is how the great institution of Plantain Hour was started. Every summer evening the rabbits have their outing in the pen, and move round from one part of the garden to another. That is why Mr. Mistletoe's lawn is now so beautiful, and why the rabbits are the most buxom in the Roslyn Estates. Just look at them!

And how about the mole subways that Donny and Fritz dug open? Well, Mr. Mistletoe had learned a great secret. It is this, that grass will always grow excellently in places where it isn't wanted or expected. The stone gutters along his driveway, and the blue gravel of the drive itself, were thick with fine healthy clumps of grass. So he invented the trick of pulling up these little clumps and transplanting them into the ragged holes where the dogs had been at work.

A grass plot could get the better of Mr. Mistletoe for a while, but it couldn't fool him permanently. In some ways he was quite an ingenious man.

By Christopher Morley

IF YOU HAD MAGIC EARS

IF YOU had magic ears, as fine as fine, so that you could hear live things growing, think what you would hear in the country of a summer's day! Every tree is making little hard buds or pushing out leaves; every tree is making all the small parts of its flowers or turning a flower into a seed pod; every tree is making its trunk a little bigger, pushing its roots a little farther into the ground. Every tree is drinking in water filled with mineral salts, sending this food in its sap up through the trunk and out into its branches, even to the very end of each leaf. Every tree is breathing, taking from the air and giving back to the air. Not only every tree; every bush, every flower, every blade of grass in the country will tell you it is growing, growing, growing.

In the city, what would you hear with your fine magic ears of a winter's day? It will not be of growing things that your ears will tell you. Their faint sounds are drowned by the clank of machinery, the thud of heavy movements, the whir of wheels. On the streets, wheels of automobiles are ever twirling, wheels of wagons ever turning; in and out of stations, on long shining rails trains are rolling on their whirling wheels; while down below the streets, whir the subway's wheels. In giant factories move smoothly the oiled wheels of great machines, cutting, turning, molding, sewing, fashioning millions of things. In great power houses revolve wheels that pump the city's water. You can hear the water running down below the city pavements where the ground is filled with pipes. Pipes for water, pipes for gas, pipes for wires—for light and power, telephone and tele-

graph—pipes for sewers, pipes for mail, pipes for steam —all down below the streets under the whirring of autos and wagons.

In more buildings more machines—clicking typewriters, adding machines, cash registers. Your keen ears can hear these millions of little clicking machines. Wheels, infinitely small wheels, buzzing quietly in all the clocks and watches; giant wheels turning quietly in the pits of steamers and ferries. A ceaseless murmur of myriads of wheels your magic ears will hear in the city. Ticking clocks, clicking typewriters, grinding derricks, winding bobbins, wheels moving on streets, under the ground, in houses and in factories. Every machine, every wheel, every moving belt in the city, will tell you it is whirring, and turning—working, working, working.

By Lucy Sprague Mitchell

TOLD
UNDER THE
BLUE UMBRELLA

Compiled by the Literature Committee

of the

ASSOCIATION FOR CHILDHOOD EDUCATION

1930–1932

Jean Betzner, Teachers College, Columbia University
Beatrice Hawksett Ireys, Minneapolis Public Schools
Frances Kern, National College of Education
Eloise Ramsey, Detroit Teachers College
Martha Seeling, Pestalozzi-Froebel Teachers College
Ethel B. Waring, New York State College of Home
Economics, Cornell University
Adah F. Whitcomb, Chicago Public Library
Mary Reed Wood, Trenton Public Schools
Chairman—Mary Lincoln Morse, Chicago Teachers
College

A MESSAGE TO GROWN UPS
BY WAY OF EXPLANATION

Told under the Blue Umbrella is presented by the Literature Committee of the Association for Childhood Education
(formerly know as the International Kindergarten Union)
as a companion volume to *Told under the Green Umbrella*.
In the fall of 1930, as a climax to the selecting story work
of the Literature Committee covering a period of ten years,
Told under the Green Umbrella was released from the
press; its special field covered the best available versions of
the best available stories with a folklore background or
imaginative approach; its stories were selected for children
of the kindergarten, first- and second-grade ages.

For many years the members of the Literature Committee, both the previous committees and the present one, have
been thoughtfully, increasingly conscious of the need of
stories for young children approaching the quality of the
folk story in character and pattern, and covering the realistic approach in imaginative treatment. Children of kindergarten age often ask of a story about to be told, "Is it
really true or is it make believe?" This shows how early
children sense the difference in the two distinct types of
imagination, that which is reproductive, or real, and that
which is combinative, or fanciful. A limited number of real
stories has always been available; stories that are on the
child way to literature, that are childlike in content, in interpretation and in pattern. Many stories of actual happenings
have been begged by eager children and told to them with
the unconscious art of the true story teller. Unfortunately
they have neither been preserved as pattern stories, as were
the folk tales, nor passed on to children other than those to
whom they were originally told. On the whole the field of
realistic stories has been and still is poverty stricken. Chal-
lenged by the need for stories of familiar experiences, of the
here and now, of stories that either are or might be possible,
the Literature Committee presents its pioneer realistic col-

lection in *Told under the Blue Umbrella*. In its age scope it has added the nursery-school age to that of the kindergarten, first- and second-grade; it includes stories for children from two to eight years of age.

The stories in *Told under the Blue Umbrella* have been sought from both outstanding and unknown writers in the field of children's literature; they have been found in both original manuscripts and in already published books for children. Every story included in *Told under the Blue Umbrella* has been considered by each committee member; while there have been differences in committee opinion, each story included has won a committee majority vote.

In looking back over the two years of digging, delving, begging for realistic stories it has been interesting to note two changes in our original committee selecting decisions. We had as a group voted to include in *Told under the Blue Umbrella* no story that was not strictly and purely realistic in imaginative treatment. This last year we again weighed this committee decision and in the light of the fact that from a story standpoint such a limitation would cut out some of the most dearly loved and best-constructed stories at our command, voted to deviate from the straight and narrow path and add to strictly real stories the nearly real ones.

Again our committee set out to include in *Told under the Blue Umbrella* only such stories as in the main deal with sufficiently universal objects and experiences to be familiar to many children in many different settings. In deviating we have added such stories as "Cinder Wagon" for instance, a story whose writing grew out of an oft-repeated winter experience of a group of nursery-school children; it was written down practically as it occurred. We realize its experience background limitations for use in many other groups at its own age level; we add it because, as a committee, we believe the shaping of such stories of vital group interest should be a story challenge to every teacher of children. It is no uncommon art, though a much needed one, to write them.

The story of "The Blue Umbrella," because of its association with our book title, has been given the first story place; the other stories follow in a general age gradation, the stories for the youngest children grouped as a whole first, for the oldest last, and for the middle-aged ones betwixt and between.

Our committee regrets its inability to secure all of the stories it selected and sought to include in *Told under the Blue Umbrella*. Copyrights were tied up, stories sought were too new in publication value to be released. (Typical of the stories chosen but not secured were "Marni Takes a Ride," "How Spot Found a Home," "The Knowing Song of the Engine" from the *Here and Now Stories,* by Lucy Sprague Mitchell.)

It was the hope of the Literature Committee members that we might secure a group of original stories dealing with that keen interest of children, the moving, working thing— the automobile, the street car, the elevated, the subway, the steam shovel, the derrick and the like. This field of machine and machinery stories is still an open one for available, individual stories of literary quality. It is quite possible that volume two of *Told under the Blue Umbrella* may be compiled in the not too far distant future when there are many more realistic stories at our disposal.

Our committee members acknowledge their appreciation to Eloise Ramsey, a committee member, for her able contribution of a brief essay on the realistic story itself; her experience in children's literature has been both intimate and wide in range. Our gratitude for the loan of original manuscripts is fittingly inscribed in a page of its own. We have dedicated another page in tribute to the friendly cooperation of both the writers of stories already published and the story publishers who granted their copyright release.

By Mary Lincoln Morse

THE EXPERIENCE STORY

A THREE-YEAR-OLD boy marked the progress of his mother's motor car through heavy traffic by half-singing to himself over and over again:

"Green light—*go*
Yellow light—*wait*
Red light—*stop*.

"Green light—*go*
Yellow light—*wait*
Red light—*stop*."

All of which is familiar enough to the ears of adults who drive cars accompanied by small active children or escort them for walks through city streets and parks. In the reiteration of these phrases we catch the swift movement of the changing traffic signals; we get the strong beat falling on "go—wait—stop." Moreover, in this bit of direct observation is the key to all that is fundamental in the realistic story of childhood experience. Here vivid motor and sensory experience in terms of color, sound, and movement bring forth spontaneous language reactions which are correspondingly rich in motor expression, rhythmic patterns and repetition. The experience has to do with a single episode in which the child is the center and chief actor, for whom the marvel of changing traffic signals repeats itself without variation. Through his pleasure in reiteration of the pattern the story gains length and gathers what it has in the way of continuity, and to the child it is satisfying because it is all his own.

Someone in search of "material for a story" listens to this rhythm and exclaims: "That fragment isn't a story. Of course children like walks and automobile rides, but in a real story their interests must be organized in a situation. Give the child character an attractive name, explain his age, for children like to be sure about the age of a child in a story, don't they? Introduce some special reason for the ride or walk—that will bring in suspense. If it is a ride,

— 155 —

show his interest in the car and have him observe the mechanical things children like. Make a good deal of the preparations for starting—that will bring in the home background. Build up detail, have him get something he wants or let him see something exciting and new, whatever it is he has been anticipating from the beginning of the story. Round it off by bringing him home thoroughly pleased with his experience. Of course the rhythm about the signals could be developed into a kind of refrain, but the main thing is plenty of action!"

Thus it is possible for the adult mind to bring confusion into a pattern of childhood experience where all was clear, colorful and satisfying.

To the child riding in the car his story happens whenever he repeats the rhythm of the signals. Another child has no place in his story.

The writer who would capture the exact quality of such a moment of experience must create imaginatively the essence of childhood itself. Herein is the explanation for the rarity with which distinction marks the realistic story of childhood experience as well as the difficulty of mastering its technique. In adult literature this has been done exquisitely in terms of memory of childhood, in delicate, wistful books in which the imaginative realization of childhood experience is sometimes almost too poignant. In the poetry children like there are amazing records of childhood moments in poetic patterns that recall the fresh voices of young children. This is the secret of the charm found by young and old in A. A. Milne's *When We Were Very Young* and Elizabeth Maddox Roberts' *Under the Tree*. This note of immediacy is what we would have for children in their stories of the here and now.

For the writer of the experience story of early childhood there are two pitfalls: the tendency to use extraneous detail and the adult conception of dramatic climax. For example, an appealing story might be developed from a child's satisfaction in making an aëroplane. If the story emphasized the work corner of the schoolroom in which the aëroplane was built, the elaboration would be adult in spirit even if it dealt with familiar things. What does the child want in the story about his own plane? As the toy wavers a moment in the air, its builder experiences supreme satisfaction. His aëroplane has conquered the air! Telling his story means getting the emotion of that moment in words.

Again, there is much confusion regarding the language of the experience story. Diligent people have recorded pages of children's talk and then announced sadly: "One can do nothing with it." Obviously, genuine experience stories are not achieved by a literal use of children's statements. The vocabulary studies of the language of young children have tended to emphasize words as words. Someone observing children in search for copy discovers that children invent words and use, amazingly enough, words that do not appear in any approved word lists! Of course this is baffling and not at all as one expected. Suggestion for the artistic interpretation of children's use of language is to be sought rather in their inflections, modulations, repetitions and rhythms—in short, in a feeling for the pattern of children's speech. The inversions and connectives which express essentially adult relationships have no part in this pattern. Likewise the generalized statement and explanatory habit of adult thought are also lacking. A successful writer of realistic stories said, "My need for relative clauses threatened the life of my stories." Clearly childhood does not offer the experiences which require an elaborate syntax for their interpretation.

The matter of children's questions presents another problem in the writing of the realistic story. With young children a question often means simply a desire for the repetition of motor rhythms which they happen to enjoy. In *Wee Ann* Ethel Calvert Phillips has shown this tendency delightfully when Wee Ann demanded of Uncle Jamie, "Tell me how the train will go tomorrow," and Uncle Jamie, always an admirable psychologist in his dealings with her, obligingly "hooted and puffed and turned himself into a train whistle."

When children wish an explanatory answer they usually make the point clear. Thus Pauline, aged six, looked puzzled during the telling of "Mr. Samson Cat," from the *Russian Picture Tales,* when she heard "Mr. Pig began to tidy up." "What does tidy mean?" she interrupted. The teacher replied: "It means to make everything neat and clean." "Oh yes, I know!" answered Pauline. "Make everything right so it won't fall out of place." Explanations which are satisfactory from the point of view of children usually have well-defined motor patterns.

The range of subject for the realistic story of childhood experience is wide enough to include all materials and activities of children. There is an impression current that the experience story is committed to the factual, not to say the literal, that it tends to deal chiefly with food, stores, post offices and transportation, that its vocabulary is determined by the requirements of early reading, that such style as it may achieve depends upon the use of tedious repetition. Unfortunately there are many pedestrian efforts of this sort now between covers, unrelieved by one flash of imagination or untouched ever so lightly with humor. They serve our purposes briefly and give place to more inspired books.

The one real limitation in the way of securing greater variety of subject and style in the writing of the experience story is that few older people can enter whole-heartedly into the imaginative life of children. It follows that highly artistic experience stories for young children are not numerous, and few of them can lay claim to the humor and gayety of the nursery rhymes and traditional tales. As the technique of the experience story grows more flexible it is hoped it may attain the spirit of fun that children love.

For the sources of art we go to life itself, and for the genuine experience story of childhood we must go directly to the children themselves, and observe the patterns they build out of their daily round of play with materials and tools, their adventures with pets, eating and sleeping. Inquiring eyes and eager hands aid them in the discovery of a wealth of meanings. The fitting of names to things becomes an intellectual adventure. Sensitive ears delight in sounds which invite repetition and encourage free experimentation with language as a medium. Out of their world of familiar sights, sounds, smells and objects large and small children establish a variety of relationships through enumeration of sounds, objects, names of persons and repetition of rhythmic phrases. The center of interest is always the child himself. In its simplest form the experience story may be a swift moment of sense impression, and even in its more developed phrases it continues episodic and lacking in climax. As children grow in maturity they gain power to appreciate sequence in narrative and come to demand more form and consequently greater variety in the manner of the experience story. When the writer can organize these experiences in motor terms, keeping at the same time a free episodic movement, the result may be a story to which children will listen with keen pleasure because they can interpret it imaginatively through their own experiences.

By Eloise Ramsey

Acknowledging the use of

STORIES ALREADY PUBLISHED

FOR permission to reprint the stories included in *Told under the Blue Umbrella* the Literature Committee of the Association for Childhood Education records its appreciation to the following:

John Day Company, New York, for the stories of "In the Grass," "Building," and "The Express Wagon," from *The Two Bobbies* by Dorothy Baruch

Doubleday, Doran and Company, Inc., Garden City, N. Y., for the story of "Rabbits with Wet Eyes," from *I Know a Secret* by Christopher Morley; "Poppy-Seed Cakes," "The Picnic Basket," "The Tea Party," from *Poppy-Seed Cakes* by Margery Clark, and "Angus and the Ducks" by Marjorie Flack

Harper and Brothers, New York, for the story of "Pelle's New Suit," by Elsa Beskow, and "A Visit to the Farm," from *In and Out with Betty Ann* by Dorothy Baruch

Houghton Mifflin Company, Boston, for the story of "Wee Ann Spends a Penny," from *Wee Ann* by Ethel Calvert Phillips

Junior Home Magazine, Chicago, for "The Story of Dobbin," by Alice Dalgliesh

Lothrop Lee and Shepherd, Boston, for the story of "The Block Tower," in *The Toy Shop* by Maud Lindsay

The Macmillan Company, New York, for the stories of "Charlie Rides in the Engine of a Real Train," from *Charlie and His Puppy Bingo* by Helen Hill and Violet Maxwell; "A Pony with a Past," from *Mercy and the Mouse* by Peggy Bacon, and "Seven White Cats," from *The Blue Tea Pot* by Alice Dalgliesh; "A City Street," "The Barn," "Ocean and Shore," and "If You Had Magic Ears," from *North America* by Lucy Sprague Mitchell

Minton Balch and Company, New York, for the story of "William and Jane," from *Jane's Father* by Dorothy Aldis

Rand McNally and Company, Chicago, for the stories of "Snow White," "The New Songs," and "Sagebrush Babies," from *Animals of a Sagebrush Ranch* by Alice Day Pratt

Row Peterson and Company, Evanston, Illinois, for "The Doll under the Briar Rosebush," from *The Birch and the Star* by Gudrun Thorne-Thomsen

Acknowledging the loan of

ORIGINAL MANUSCRIPTS

FOR the generous loan of original stories never before published, some of which were written by request, some thoughtfully offered for use if need be, the Literature Committee of the Association for Childhood Education records its gratitude to the following:

Marie Louise Allen, for the story of "Jim and Scotch and the Little Red Wagon"

Marjorie Allen Anderson, for the story of "Little Sheep One, Two, Three"

Marjorie Hardy, for the story of "Big Tree"

Mabel G. LaRue, for the story of "The Jack-o'-Lantern"

Helen Fuller Orton, for the story of "The Dinner Bell"

Mary G. Phillips, for the stories of "Paddy's Three Pets," and "The Feel of Things"

Katharine Reeves, for the stories of "Roxy and the Robin," "The Cinder Wagon," and "Walking in the Woods"

Frances Rowley, for the story of "Lost in the Leaves"

James Tippett, for the story of "The Blue Umbrella"